THE FRENCH GRADUATE

Book 1

By
Kenneth Chang

The French Graduate

Copyright © 2025

Dedication

This book is dedicated to my "Angeli," who is a constant source of inspiration and love in my life. I am grateful for everything you do.

To everyone, living or dead, who has helped shape my life—this is for you.

Acknowledgment

    I want to thank everyone who has been a part of my journey. Your support and encouragement have helped me in many ways. To my family, friends, and mentors, thank you for being there for me and for believing in me. Your influence has meant a lot to me.

Kenneth Chang

Kenny Cannon is an enigma in his own moment in time. He lives in a modest urban town in Connecticut, where his family falls somewhere between rich and poor. His parents, Henry and Sylvia, are not college graduates. Henry has a well-paying job, while Sylvia is a stay-at-home mom who engages in charitable work whenever possible.

From a young age, Kenny exhibits intelligence, which he believes is inherited from a wise and perceptive ancestor, though he has never explored his genealogy to confirm this. This perceived ancestral wisdom occasionally manifests as Kenny grows up, helping him achieve good, though not extraordinary, grades. His teachers have never pushed him, and he completes assignments with a lack of inspiration.

However, in his senior year, Kenny's grades plummeted, a fact unknown to his parents, who assume he is performing as well as before. His grades are poor across all subjects, including an "F" in his elective French class taught by Mr. Woods, a married and dedicated teacher.

Kenny has been part of a gang since freshman year, led by Ben with two other members, Allen and Glen. While they all have licenses, only Ben owns a car. Kenny borrows his parents' car for special occasions. The group shares a deep bond, being good-natured, loyal, and lifelong friends. Glen is the jokester, Allen is the handyman, and Kenny is the intellectual one.

Kenny finds himself confronting a personal conundrum regarding his grades and his overall ambivalence towards his current life. He reaches a significant conclusion: his virginity is the root cause of his troubles. Kenny has no girlfriend, no knowledge of girls, no sexual experiences, and no sisters to interact with, leaving him clueless about the female gender. This lack of experience, which he shares with his gang, weighs heavily on him.

The French Graduate

Determined to address the issue, Kenny brings it up with his friends. "Look, guys, I don't know about you, but I'm tired of being a virgin. I need to get laid. We all do; we're all in the same boat."

Ben snorts. "Well, that's easy to say, but with no girlfriends, and the girls we know don't even give us the time of day. Only Britta seems to like you, Kenny, but she doesn't seem the type to put out. I could be wrong."

"No, you're right," Kenny confirms. "Britta is a nice girl, and I like her. I don't think she's the type. She must be a virgin like us."

"Okay, smart ass, what are we going to do? Go to a whorehouse?" Allen laughs.

"Well, don't hold your breath," Kenny chimes in. "This is not Vegas."

"It's legal there, but there must be something we can do. Ben, didn't you mention something about it way back?" Kenny asked.

"You're right," Ben replied. "Now that it's relevant, I remember hearing something about it here in town. I wasn't interested back then. I know who mentioned it, but finding him might be tricky. I see him around sometimes. Let me check it out. This could be our solution, Kenny."

"I hope it's not just rumors. Right here in town, huh? Give me a couple of days, and I'll find him," Ben assured. "You won't die even if I don't find him. But don't worry, if he's gone, someone else will know. If it existed once, it probably still does."

"Well, keep in mind that my life and grades depend on it," Kenny confided.

On the third day, after two days of dead ends, Ben came back with good news. "Not the guy I knew, but his friend. They both went there. It's a private type of brothel, very selective and discreet. That's why it's almost under our noses. I checked it out. It's on 3rd Street, house number 27, at the very end, with good parking. Saturday is the most logical day. We can't go at night; it has to be sometime in the afternoon."

"We're not exactly invited. If we just show up, they'll probably think it was a referral. We'll have to take a chance. It will be broad daylight, so we need to be discreet. No clown masks, Glen," Kenny joked.

"Is there a plan B?" Allen asked.

"Right now, no. I'm just hoping all goes well. Keep your fingers crossed," Kenny replied.

Saturday came sooner than expected. It was their game plan, do-or-die time, with their motto: to get laid. They also hoped that the fifty bucks each had would be enough. Ben never asked how much it would cost. The time of reckoning was now, and Ben picked up the gang. Everyone had an anxious, apprehensive look. They stopped a few houses away to survey number 27. The house was well-kept and landscaped, with an inviting but discreet appearance. Slightly larger than the surrounding houses, it looked normal in all respects.

This brothel, run by a madam for selective clientele, served regular customers from the community and rarely outsiders. Unlike regular brothels, this one had a unique dynamic. There was a special relationship between the madam and one of the prostitutes, Patey. Some clients sought therapy alongside sex.

Ben parked, and they exited the car, trying to appear normal. A small sign read, "Please ring first, then enter." The gang filed in and sat in a comfortable parlor. The room was neatly decorated, with a sweet fragrance permeating the air. They waited nervously, exchanging glances and watching for someone to greet them. Unbeknownst to them, a camera in the parlor allowed the madam and Patey to observe them from another location. Patey, the only prostitute with a monitor, informed the madam of her choice or lack thereof. This arrangement worked well for everyone involved.

Patey, 25, was a beautiful blonde and an intelligent, one-of-a-kind prostitute. Born to a wealthy family in France, she attended university for two years, studying philosophy and psychiatry, before deciding to travel and learn from other cultures. She ended up at this brothel, bringing her unique skill set with her. Patey spoke fluent French and was known as the therapeutic prostitute, offering therapeutic sex. She intended to move on in life eventually.

As the gang sat waiting, they observed a group of scantily dressed girls chatting with an older woman and one in a white velvet robe. One by one, a prostitute approached and chose a boy to follow her, except for Kenny. Left alone, Kenny wondered what was going on. Did they forget about him? Were they short-handed? Was he dressed wrong? Had he parted his hair the wrong way? What was it?

Then, the woman in the white robe approached Kenny. "Hi, handsome, I'm Patey. I'll be your host. Come here often?" Patey extended her hand with a gentle touch, a gesture Kenny had never experienced from someone so beautiful. It sent a shiver of delight through him, a pulse of electricity he could barely describe. He froze for a moment. "Just kidding. Come with me, please," Patey said, coaxing Kenny down a hall to her room.

"I'm inviting you to my chambers. Enter at your peril," Patey laughed. Kenny walked into an immaculate setting. A beige, low-profile rug covered the floor. At the center of the room was a beautiful king-size bed with pink sheets and three lavender pillows. To the left was a makeup dresser with a round mirror surrounded by lights. Further left was a monitor on a table and a small table with two chairs. To the right was a wardrobe closet and, further on, a door to a bathroom. Behind the bed was a dimmer switch. Patey climbed onto the bed to soften the lighting, and as she slid off to the side, Kenny glimpsed her red panties and bra.

Instead of standing in front of him, Patey sat next to him. "What do you prefer that I call you?" Patey whispered.

"Kenny. It's my real name. And you're Patey. Simply Patey. Okay. What happens now? I'm a little nervous," Kenny admitted.

"Well, first, do you mind if I ask you a few questions?" Patey asked, looking directly at him.

"No, but I don't know anything about nuclear fission or the distance to Pluto," Kenny joked.

Patey laughed loudly. "Well, it seems everyone wants to be a comedian," she responded. "Yes, go ahead," she continued slowly. "Do you have a girlfriend, and are you a virgin?"

"Well, it's no to the first one and yes to the second. But I'm hoping to fix that, I hope."

Patey smiled. "Yes, I can fix that. But if you don't mind, again, I'm a little curious about you. Can you give me a little synopsis of yourself? I get a sense of complexity, so I'm curious."

Kenny was puzzled. He came there for sex, but instead, it felt like a question-and-answer session and now his whole life story. Is this how it normally goes? I'd ask Ben if this happened to him, too. The pause created by his thoughts left him with a blank stare.

Patey smiled and reassured him, "It's not compulsory."

"No, no, I don't mind at all. It just caught me by surprise. I've never been asked, especially by a beautiful woman. O-boy, let me gather my thoughts on this. I'm not an Einstein, but I do have a very perceptive mind. I somehow believe that my DNA from past ancestors endowed me with this perceptive mind and passed it on to me. Why me and why now, I don't know. I perceive things differently than others, but I don't tell anyone. I keep it to myself. I'm an only child, so I don't know much about girls."

The French Graduate

"In school, I'm a senior and have always had good grades, but now I'm embarrassed to tell you that my grades have dropped in all my subjects. I even have an 'F' in French, which I'll never need or use in my life. I have no interest in the subject at all, and signing up for it was a mistake. I might be wrong, but I somehow think my low grades are because I'm a virgin. It feels like sex is the missing ingredient in my drive. My lack of interest in school might be because my libido is in overdrive. What do you think? Ahh...don't answer that. It might be biased.

I belong to a gang, as you might have noticed, in the parlor. Ben, Allen, and Glen are my friends. We've been close for years and always have each other's backs. They're loyal friends, a little rough around the edges, but great guys. They're all virgins like me. We came here to maybe change that."

Patey listened and then said, "I don't think your friends are going to change that status. As you talked, I saw them being escorted out from that monitor. It views the parlor. How much money did each of you have?"

Kenny reached into his pocket and replied, "I have more, but they each had fifty dollars."

Patey laughed, pushing Kenny's money away. "Your perception is way off. We're not cheap. We are a high-end establishment. That monitor over there, only I have one. It's an arrangement I'm granted. It is hooked up to the greeting lounge. I am the only one who can choose my client, and my regulars choose me. I am their therapeutic prostitute. I try to solve their problems if they have any. Sex and therapy are not cheap. I help with their problems in life and, of course, sex, but not all the time. We talk like I'm doing with you.

I'm also an only child. I grew up in France. My parents are wealthy and very liberal, providing me with the best education. I went through high school and spent two years at a French university studying philosophy and psychology. I decided to travel to other countries to learn more about life first-hand, and that brought me here. Aren't you lucky? I speak perfect, fluent French. Let me give you a taste of it."

Patey spoke in French exquisitely and eloquently.

"Who would think? A prostitute with culture, philosophy, and fluent French. You are something else, one of a kind. I'm in love with you already. Marry me, and I'll leave my three wives and ten kids for you," Kenny joked.

Patey laughed and responded, "Yes, and I need a comedian. Laughter is good for the soul, and that's why I selected you. You looked like a clown. How's that for a rejoinder?"

It was so odd to hear hearty laughter coming from the room instead of moans. "I like you too, Kenny. We make a good comedy team," Patey said as their laughter slowed down. She then stiffened and declared, "Life is not all fun and games. We need to get serious about the situation."

As Kenny sat silently on the edge of the bed, Patey seemed to be in deep thought, almost in a trance.

Patey's thoughts raced. "I like this guy. He's smart and funny, wants to get laid, and is failing in his grades, especially French, which I'm good at. There must be a solution that's a win/win for everyone, including me. Maybe fate designed this to happen—Kenny, me, French, sex, life! Why don't I become Kenny's mentor and make him learn French by ruse? He needs to be motivated to learn it. The motivation can be his expectation of getting sex. I'll bait him with the promise of sex if he asks me for it in French. I'll keep refusing him each time, even when he gets it right. However, I'll need to placate him with something sensual and erotic, like a hug, kiss, undress, and so on, so he doesn't lose interest or discover the ruse. I'm sure I can come up with something. This plan doesn't entail intercourse, but I

The French Graduate

don't think that will be necessary for the end game. This will be a game changer for everyone, including me. I can feel it," Patey concluded.

"Kenny, I'm going to make you an offer you can't refuse. I'm not going to charge you a fee for sex that you couldn't afford on one condition: you come back here and ask me for sex in good grammatical French. Do you think you can handle that? Come back here when you are ready, and I will tell them to let you in to see me. But be warned, don't take too long. I may change my mind."

Kenny didn't have to think about it; his answer was quick, "Yes. Please don't change your mind. I'll be back before the cock crows twice," he said, trying to impress Patey. "I'm on it. You won't regret it," Kenny boasted.

As Kenny started to get up, Patey stood in front of him, leaned over, and kissed him on his cheek. Not just a peck but a deliberate, lingering kiss. This was a first for Kenny—a woman kissed him. Wow!

Since the gang was gone, he could have walked home but decided to phone Ben to pick him up and to ask him some questions. It was still early evening, so Kenny's mom would assume that the gang must have eaten something somewhere. Ben arrived, not only with the car but with questions. "What went on for so long with Patey?" Ben asked the name Kenny gave to the prostitute he was with.

Kenny couldn't stop talking about Patey. "She was awesome, brilliant, beautiful, and funny. She was my Holy Grail. She's going to give me sex."

Ben interjected, "Wait, what do you mean going to? Didn't you get laid? Hours with a prostitute and nothing? Only talk? I hope you didn't pay her."

"Ben, it's complicated. We're running out of time. I will tell you all about it later, I promise." A wave goodbye was his consolation prize, knowing that Allen and Glen also wanted to hear it.

Kenny took a shower but tried not to wash the spot that Patey kissed. If he could, he would frame it. He slept with a contented feeling.

The next day was Sunday. Kenny's family weren't practicing Catholics, so they only attended mass on special occasions like Christmas or Easter, dragging Kenny along on those days. Sunday was a catch-all day for doing whatever needed to be done or even nothing at all. Usually, something needed fixing or working on, and Kenny was good at fixing things. If the task was huge, the gang helped out.

After dinner, Kenny decided to open his French book and study into the night. He knew that tomorrow would be a day full of questions from the gang between classes and after school. They couldn't wait to question him, and Kenny couldn't wait to tell them every detail.

"You're not going to believe what happened. I'm still in euphoria. This gal, the prostitute Patey, is awesome. She's everything. She's beautiful, intelligent, insightful, perceptive, went to a university in France, traveled, and guess what? She speaks perfect French. But no, we did not have sex. When I left, she kissed me right here," Kenny pointed to his cheek and swooned. "I could feel her body and her presence when she kissed me. I thought I would melt. But maybe next time, I might get luckier. Maybe sex. You don't know it, but Patey has a monitor in her room. She watched you guys being escorted out. Sorry about that."

They listened intently, wondering if it could have been them instead. "But there's a catch to getting it on with Patey. She wants me to sort of beg her for it in French. Me, with my low grades in French—I'll never get laid."

Ben and Allen both encouraged Kenny to ask the French teacher Mr. Woods to come up with a phrase for asking for it in French. "It's certainly worth a try. I'd do it in a heartbeat. Can I take your place for you?"

The French Graduate

"Oh, come on. You don't know anything about French," Kenny retorted, but it gave him food for thought. How lucky he was to get this chance that others could only wish for. Kenny gave a thumbs up and boasted, "I'm in."

They all laughed and gave Kenny a thumbs up, too, as they left.

The next day in French class, Kenny was extra attentive and eager to talk to Mr. Woods. He was a little embarrassed to relate his bravado episode with Patey. Mr. Woods just smiled, probably reminiscing about his own youth. His chuckling gave Kenny the impression that he wasn't going to be too judgmental.

Mr. Woods thought to himself, "This might be the spark Kenny needs to learn his French. I also don't think Kenny is unaware of this ruse. Kenny praises Patey as being intelligent and having studied philosophy. I think she's playing a game with him to learn French. I'm certainly not going to tell him. I could never motivate him at all, but sex sells, they say."

Mr. Woods expressed a twinkling smile of approval. "Kenny," Mr. Woods said, "I'm good with it. I'll work out a phrase in French for you to try, but it's up to you to learn and practice it. I hope it works for you. Let me know how it went. I'll have it ready for you tomorrow."

Kenny thanked him and left to meet with the gang before going home.

The next day, Kenny received the French phrases from Mr. Woods and practiced them, still struggling to pronounce them correctly. For the rest of the week, Kenny rehearsed tirelessly, even trying to get help from the gang, who couldn't offer much assistance. With Saturday approaching rapidly, he knew he wasn't proficient enough, but he didn't want Patey to change her mind about their deal.

On Saturday, Ben picked up Kenny, who was nervous and jittery. Ben tried to calm him down before dropping him off at the brothel. As Kenny walked in, he was directed towards Patey's room. Patey, who had been watching Kenny on her monitor, stood at the door before he even had a chance to knock.

"Hi, Kenny. Come in. I've been waiting for you. Did I appear in your dreams?" Patey greeted him warmly. "I have some ginger ale for you—no liquor, sorry. There's a table for two; sit there. But before we get started, can we talk a bit? I'd like to know more about you. Do you drink alcohol, do drugs, have a criminal record, or anything else I should know? If you answer yes to any of these, you're out of here before we continue."

Kenny was taken aback by the questions. Morality? Integrity? At a brothel? "I'll confess," he said, "No to all of those, but thanks for asking."

"I figured as much, but it doesn't hurt to check. I don't usually ask these questions, only on special occasions. So, you're special—rejoice," Patey said with a smile. "I want to ask you more, but that can wait. For now, it's time for some ale."

Patey returned with a tray of ice-cold ginger ale and poured it into two glasses. "Wow," Kenny thought, "this is class." Trying to be suave, he clinked Patey's glass and said, "Here's to the French goddess."

"Thank you, Kenny," Patey replied, chuckling. "But you're already a bit tipsy from the ginger ale. It must be the bubbles. I appreciate the gesture; you're so thoughtful."

Then, out of the blue, Patey asked, "How's your mom?"

Kenny was surprised. It felt oddly personal. "She's fine. It's a pleasant surprise to be asked about her. It never occurred to me that anyone would phrase it that way. That was really nice. Maybe you'll meet her sometime. Just so you know, she doesn't know about you. Not because you're bad, but... it's complicated."

Patey touched the rim of her glass to Kenny's lips and said, "I understand. I have a mom, too, and I know what it's like. Finish your ale before it gets warm. By the way, what kind of music do you like? I'm a fan of the old-timers—Frank Sinatra, Perry Como, Paul Anka, Andy Williams. And you?"

"The same," Kenny replied. "I also like country and western, especially the old-timers like Hank Williams. His songs have meaning. It seems we have a lot in common."

"Well, let's take it one step at a time," Patey said. "Finish your ale, and let's get started."

Patey slid onto the bed, adjusted the dimmer to lower the lights, and murmured, "How's your French coming along?" She was keen not to lose sight of her goal with Kenny. His heart raced, and a lump formed in his throat; he knew his French wasn't polished. But what if it was good enough? Kenny sat there, lost in thought, feeling like a zombie. Isn't this supposed to be spontaneous?

As Patey reclined on a pillow, pulling aside part of her robe to reveal her red bra and a hint of red panties, Kenny felt overwhelmed. He was at the point of no return and had no idea how to handle the situation. How could he get aroused when his mind was consumed with French phrases? With no answers, Kenny stood up to face Patey, who was lying provocatively on the bed. Nervously, he fumbled with the top button of his shirt. Patey raised her hand in a stopping motion and said, "Are you going to tell me what you want in French?"

Kenny's mind raced, his entire life flashing before him. What should he say? What should he do? He felt like he might either melt or burst into tears. In a moment of panic, he put his hands on his face, covered his eyes, and sobbed. He sat down on the edge of the bed, avoiding Patey's gaze.

"Sorry, Patey, I'm lost," he said, his voice trembling. "I forgot the words. I'm just... I'm such a mess."

Patey curled up next to Kenny, cradled his head on her chest, and patted his shoulder, comforting him in silence. She understood his predicament but also knew that, given the circumstances, he wasn't going to get laid anyway. The poor thing, Patey thought with sympathy. She recognized that Kenny wasn't ready to learn the language in such a short time and that his virginity made the situation even more challenging. It was clear to Patey that Kenny's lack of progress was expected, and she felt a sense of satisfaction in managing the situation, even if it was at his expense.

"I'm so sorry," Kenny said, still sobbing a bit.

"Don't be," Patey replied. "You did well under the circumstances. It was a tough assignment. I'd give you an 'A' for effort," she added with a laugh.

Kenny, not in a cheerful mood, responded, "I deserve an 'F.'"

"Okay, then an 'F+,'" Patey said, giggling.

"Not funny," Kenny snorted. "I'll commit hari-kari if you don't mind."

Patey smirked slightly, and they both hugged each other, laughing heartily.

"You're wonderful, Patey," Kenny said, still feeling a bit shaken but grateful. "Even with all this, you made me feel good and helped me save face. I hope you'll give me another chance. Now that I've calmed down let me try my French statement." He took a deep breath and recited his lines.

Patey smiled, then frowned, and said, "Sorry, Kenny, but with that, you'll never make it to first base. You'll need to do better if you want to get to second, third, or even score a home run. If you catch my drift."

"Not a good deal for me," Kenny said. "I didn't get to tell you that I'm not really into sports."

"Kenny, it was just a metaphor, so don't get your underwear in a bunch. Or is that another metaphor?" Patey replied with a smile. "Anyway, it's good to learn more about you. Even though you didn't do well, you made an effort despite the distractions. I hate to cut your session short, but I want you to get home at a decent hour for your mom. Before you go, I should let you know that I don't live here full-time. I have an apartment in town. Here's my address and phone number—always call me first; never assume anything. I want you to come to my apartment, but I expect you to be a more polished gentleman and level-headed next time, okay?"

"If you remember, last time I gave you a treat for your efforts in French. I have another one for you now. Close your eyes and keep your mouth shut."

Patey stood up from the bed and positioned herself in front of Kenny, who was sitting on the edge with his eyes closed, wondering what his reward would be. She gently kissed his closed lips very sensually. Kenny felt her soft lips and opened his eyes to see Patey's face close to his. The kiss lasted about two seconds, but it felt like an eternity to him.

"Wow, that was something else. I never imagined what a kiss would feel like," Kenny said, a bit dazed. "Do it again."

Patey could have easily told him no, but she found the moment interesting and precious for both of them. "Alright, I'll do it again, but just this once, and then you need to go home," she said with a smile.

Kenny closed his eyes again, his anticipation building. He could sense her presence close to him and thought about reaching out but hesitated. What if she stopped him? Patey sensed his hesitation and guided his hands gently to her hips, instructing him to hold her lightly.

With his eyes still closed, Kenny felt her body moving under his fingers. Patey leaned forward and kissed him again, this time a bit longer. He relaxed and savored the full experience of being kissed by a woman. When Patey finally pulled away, Kenny's eyes remained closed in a state of euphoria.

"Kenny, wake up," Patey said gently. "Sorry to break your bubble, but we had a deal, right? I kept my end of it, so now it's time for you to go. Your mom is waiting."

Kenny got off the bed and joked, "I'm a little tipsy—can you get drunk on kisses? I have to admit, this has been one hell of a day for me." He seemed reluctant to leave.

Patey was pleased that her mentoring plan was working well. She was confident that Kenny, excited by the experience, would be motivated to study his French diligently. Not wanting to upset Patey was clearly a priority for him.

Days turned into a week. Kenny worked hard on his subjects and focused intensively on French. He even crafted his own solicitation for sex in French, hoping to impress Patey. "Maybe this time," he mused. It had been just one week since he had experienced the thrill of a lifetime. But what if it had been sex instead of just a kiss? How would that feel? He wondered if he could handle it. Just thinking about it made him anxious; he worried he might not survive the experience. Each day, he diligently completed his assignments and volunteered to speak French, earning giggles from the girls in class. Mr. Woods encouraged Kenny's increased participation, which did not go unnoticed by the gang. They observed Kenny spending more time on class material and with Mr. Woods.

Kenny was aware of their slight reactions and apologized for joining them late. He would always regale them with details about his time with Patey, which led to playful teasing from his friends. "Trust me, you guys, you'd disintegrate and self-destruct," Kenny said with a grin, though he couldn't help but wonder if they might have handled it better than he did. Despite his emotional turmoil, he felt more confident with each interaction with Patey. She was undeniably cool.

Previously, Kenny had spent a lot of time with his gang, but lately, he had been more focused on schoolwork and his new relationship—his first serious one. Normally, he would be with his friends on Saturday mornings until 3 p.m. After that, he reserved time for Patey. She managed their time together, always mindful of Kenny's mom's schedule and concerns. Patey's approach was straightforward: she gave Kenny his marching orders, making it clear that he had to comply. It wasn't a matter of negotiation. Kenny wasn't just a passive participant in her plan, though.

As Saturday approached, Kenny was up early. His mom was surprised to see him awake before she started breakfast. She had noticed him studying something and shrugged it off as she prepared the meal. At the breakfast table, Kenny's mom nudged him and said, "You've been studying a lot lately. I heard you mumbling something in French. How's that going? You used to complain about it. I can't really help you with that, even if I wanted to. Are you seeing your friends today? I haven't seen or talked to them in a while. Tell them I said hello and to have a good day. They're good guys. Invite them over sometime. If you're in a hurry, just go. For dinner, we're having spaghetti with French bread. How's that for a contribution?" She laughed, and Kenny smiled at her response. At least she was supportive.

Of course, Kenny's mom had no idea that he wasn't spending all his time with the gang or that he was seeing Patey regularly and practicing French to use with her in hopes of a sexual encounter. Kenny felt a twinge of guilt but pushed it aside. He couldn't give up Patey, whether out of love or a deeper feeling that she was going to change his life. He felt it was his destiny to continue seeing her. Losing Patey was simply not an option in Kenny's mind.

Around 3 p.m., Ben drops Kenny off near Patey's place. It's close enough for Kenny to walk, but he's with the gang, so it's easier this way. The guys blow kisses at him, teasing him as he heads inside. Kenny rushes upstairs to Patey's apartment, grinning with excitement. His smile widens even more when he sees Patey waiting at the door, her face alight with a warm, inviting smile. She greets him with an embrace and a kiss on the lips, which startles him slightly, but he strives to remain calm and receptive, even though the kiss stirs a whirlwind of emotions inside him.

"Hi, babe," Kenny says, trying to sound casual. "You look wonderful. Less is more," he adds with a chuckle. Patey is dressed in a light blue robe with a pink bra and panties, although they're not visible. The robe is tied in front, adding to her allure.

"Let's have some ale again," Patey suggests. "But if you'd prefer something else, let me know. Do you have a favorite drink?"

"No, ale is perfect," Kenny replies. "I really like it. But you're spoiling me with how chilled this is. It's a nice contrast to the warm weather outside. You're so thoughtful."

"I knew you enjoyed it the first time," Patey says with a smile. "It was a no-brainer to offer it again. I look forward to our time together. I feel good knowing you're coming. I've been waiting for you."

As Kenny sips his chilled drink, he reflects on Patey's words. He marvels at the way she makes him feel—how her presence sends shivers down his spine and fills him with joy. He feels like she truly understands him and touches his heart in a way no one else does. It's as if she has the power to make everything in his world glow. He wonders if this is love or simply the feeling of being in love. His emotions are overwhelming, a rapid rush of sensations that seem to occur in the blink of an eye.

"Patey," Kenny says, hesitating, "do you have feelings for me? I'm not just a client or a number, am I? You haven't accepted any money from me, and you invite me back openly. You seem to care. Why is that? Is it because I speak French? Or is there something else?"

Patey reaches across the table and gently touches Kenny's hand. "Kenny, I'll confess, there's something about you that fascinates me. You have a quality that genuinely excites me. I need you just as much as you need me. While you seek a physical connection, I'm looking for emotional support. I need guidance and someone to help steer my future."

"Kenny, please understand," she continues, "I have certain goals that I'm working towards, and you don't need to know the specifics. This experience is new and overwhelming for both of us. You're infatuated with me, but I sense that there's more to your feelings than just physical attraction. My personality can be intense, and I have feelings too. You came into my life at just the right moment. I hope I'm not confusing you. If it makes you happy, I'll say it plainly: I love you… in my own way."

Kenny absorbs every word Patey says, his mind racing to process her heartfelt confession. He looks deeply into her eyes, trying to make sense of it all. "You're saying that you love me in your own way. I don't even know what love is for me. You're in my every thought. I don't know what real love is. We share our feelings, but is this true love? If it isn't, I don't care; I can't stop. You are irresistible to me. You're all I think about."

Kenny, struggling to articulate his thoughts, asks, "But will this last? Will we get tired of each other?"

Patey laughs softly and replies, "That's not an option. Our DNA is practically married—no divorce."

A little later, Kenny adds, "Well, this is an interesting revelation. And I haven't even made my French proposal to you yet. Prepare to be blown away." As they move away from the small table, Patey leaps onto the bed, shuffling the lavender pillows. She reclines on one of them, opening her robe to reveal her beautiful body, though still covered by her bra and panties. Kenny approaches the bed, kneeling and unbuttoning his top button, trying to look suave as he recites his French composition.

However, Patey knows she must stick to the plan. She gracefully declines, not wanting to hurt Kenny's feelings. She giggles lightly, then draws her robe closed and ties it. Sitting up and placing a pillow on her lap, she says, "I like the wording—it has a lot of meaning. But some of the pronunciations weren't quite right today. However, we'll still reward you for your efforts. You can take off your shirt and lie down on that pillow. Keep your pants on, though."

Kenny, always in socks indoors while Patey prefers being barefoot, snuggles his head into the pillow, his mind racing with anticipation about his reward. Patey crawls over to his side, opens her robe slightly, and places her body against his chest. She whispers, "You can open your mouth now. I'm going to French kiss you."

Kenny's thoughts evaporate as Patey covers his lips with hers. He feels her warm body pressed against his chest and her warm lips on his. Their lips blend together, and an unusual sensation fills him as Patey's tongue gently enters his mouth, creating a deliciously sensual feeling. Unsure of how to respond, Kenny simply melts into the pillow.

As Patey pulls away and sits up, she asks, "How did the French go? Interested in learning more?"

"It was incredible," Kenny replies, his voice filled with awe. "It was like the Fourth of July on my lips, but I didn't know how to respond. It was my first time, but you knew that. Thank you so much, Patey. I hope we do it again."

The French Graduate

As they both slide to the edge of the bed, Kenny reaches for his shirt and starts to put it on. Patey moves in front of him and says, "Here, let me button it up for you. Next time, I'll take it off," with a playful smile.

Kenny grins and responds, "You have my permission to do anything you want with me. I've already signed my consent form in my back pocket." They share a laugh, enjoying each other's jokes.

"Okay, off to Mom. See you next week, and don't forget your lessons—both school and here."

Without thinking, Kenny heads toward the door to say goodbye. Patey walks up to him and says, "Why don't you show me what you've learned today?" Kenny, momentarily blank, thinks, What a dummy, I didn't even think of a goodbye kiss. He says, "Sorry, I was still vibrating. Yes, I'd like that." Kenny embraces Patey and gives her a French kiss, albeit an amateurish one. Patey gives him a thumbs-up and waves him off with a smile.

There was no longer any doubt that Kenny was fully committed to his studies and had developed a renewed enthusiasm for life. It felt like an epiphany of sorts. His favorite subject now was French, and when he talked to his gang, the conversation inevitably turned to kissing, kissing, kissing, and French kissing. They must have asked him over five times and still wanted to know more. They listened intently, with a mix of jealousy and empathy.

Not that Kenny was excessively talkative about Patey—she was a fictional figure, after all, and no one knew otherwise. Even Mr. Woods found Kenny's newfound motivation intriguing and understood that Patey's influence was a significant factor in Kenny's drive to learn French. This newfound respect extended to how Kenny viewed the girls in his classes; he now saw them in a different light. To disrespect women, he realized, would be to disrespect Patey. As a result, the girls began engaging in small talk with Kenny, who had also gained the counselor Mr. Weston's approval, receiving a thumbs-up whenever their paths crossed. Everything seemed to be falling into place, and Kenny hoped it wasn't just an illusion.

Kenny couldn't shake the feeling that so many changes were washing over him, like waves crashing at the edge of his consciousness. He replayed moments of bewilderment and the exhilaration of a French kiss, wondering if it was all just a dream or hallucination. He concluded it couldn't be—he could still feel her tongue, lips, and body. There was no "delete" button for these sensations in his mind.

He found it hard not to fantasize a little. What would his next treat be? It had escalated from a peck to a French kiss. Kenny thought about bringing Patey flowers or even a single rose. He should have thought of this sooner. She had been so generous to him; he wanted to reciprocate. The idea of giving her something made him feel good.

For Kenny, each day was a new challenge. He needed to balance his commitment to improving his grades and mastering French. Fortunately, Patey was a compelling incentive, and he hoped one day to have a conversation with her in French. Each day presented its own hurdles, but he managed to find solace with his gang, who helped him unwind with new jokes from Glen, easing his stress. He felt he might implode if not for their support.

The gang was just as curious about Patey as Kenny was. They often asked, "What's next, Kenny? I bet you can't wait for Saturday, huh? You must be anxious, but you seem so calm and calculated. Are you losing interest in Patey?" Kenny thought for a moment before responding, "No, not at all. It's just that Patey has certain expectations of me, and I don't want to disappoint her. I know I've stumbled before, but I'm working on it. It takes time, so I'm stretching out the days to polish my French and address other things as well. Saturday will come soon enough. Patey is certainly the highlight, but give it a rest, okay?"

The French Graduate

The gang seemed frustrated that Saturday wasn't arriving faster, but as Kenny knew, the earth's rotation was fixed and couldn't be sped up.

Despite Kenny's efforts to focus on his family, school, French, and his gang, his thoughts frequently drift back to Patey. He would often try to push these thoughts aside to concentrate on other matters. Even before he falls asleep, his mind gravitates towards Patey, and every time he attempts to imagine what's next, he drifts off. He admits that there are so many possibilities that it feels futile, and sleep provides a much-needed escape from his relentless thoughts.

Day by day, Kenny faces and resolves various issues, though his life feels increasingly crowded. However, Patey remains a comforting presence amidst his anxieties. Speaking with Mr. Woods, a mature married man, offers him valuable perspective. Sometimes, Mr. Woods playfully chides Kenny, suggesting that his marital experience adds an extra edge to his advice, which always gives them both a good laugh. Mr. Woods is genuinely pleased with Kenny's progress in French class and congratulates him on his efforts, even if Patey doesn't accept his composition intended to seduce her. It seems that Kenny's romantic life has piqued Mr. Woods's and the gang's interest, and the anticipation for the week ahead is palpable. Even Kenny himself is eagerly awaiting Saturday, though he tries to temper his excitement.

Kenny's mom remains puzzled and curious about his behavior. She bombards him with questions: "Kenny, are you in love with someone? Do you have a girlfriend? Are you seeing someone? How do you want me to put it, seriously? If there is someone, when will you introduce her to us?" Kenny just smiles and shrugs it off. "Then it must be true. You're trying to hide it; otherwise, you'd admit it. You're being sneaky," she remarks. Kenny departs, still smiling slyly.

Kenny's mom grows increasingly suspicious of his cheerful demeanor, especially after asking about a girlfriend. She wonders if he finally has one, as she has been concerned about him spending so much time with his friends. She thinks any girl would be a good match for him. Intrigued and curious, she decides to investigate further. She doubts that Kenny will have time for a girl between classes, so she plans to check after school when he might meet up with someone.

Mom parks a little way from the school's parking lot, hoping to see Kenny with a girl without making it obvious that she is spying. She chuckles to herself, thinking that this is a harmless bit of undercover work. As school lets out and students begin to disperse, she spots Kenny with his gang, but no girl in sight. Disappointed, she mutters to herself, "I guess I was wrong. I should head home."

Just then, she notices Kenny pointing towards someone in the distance. A beautiful blonde woman wearing dark glasses in a red convertible pulls up to the curb where Kenny and his friends are standing. Kenny waves at her, opens the car door, and gets in. The girl waves back at the gang and then drives away, her hair blowing in the wind with Kenny beside her. Mom is puzzled: Is she his girlfriend? A friend? An Uber driver? Why are the gang members whistling and cheering? A blonde girlfriend with a red convertible? Mom wonders if she is a young teacher or someone special. Confused and not wanting to confront Kenny immediately, she decides it might just be a fluke, though she is certain it is not Britta.

Back at home, Mom casually asks Kenny, "How was your day? Met any interesting girls lately? You seemed to have a secret smile the last time I asked." Kenny responds with a grin, "Nope, no new girls." Mom immediately regrets her choice of words, realizing that the girl she saw looked a bit older than Kenny. It seems he wasn't lying, just avoiding the topic. Determined to uncover more, Mom decides to go undercover again.

However, it turns out that Patey doesn't pick Kenny up every day—only occasionally when she can. So Mom waits by the school but doesn't see the red convertible. Disappointed, she resolves to give it one more day.

The French Graduate

The next day, fate intervenes. Mom waits, feeling a bit perplexed when the red convertible swings by once again. Kenny waves enthusiastically, his gang playfully poking him in the ribs. The same blonde woman with dark glasses smiles and gives a friendly wave from the driver's seat as Kenny gets in. Mom takes note of the details: Patey is a bit older than Kenny, around 25, blonde, very beautiful, and well-dressed. This woman seems impressive, and Mom wonders who she might be.

As Patey drives away with Kenny, Mom is left with more information and a sense of intrigue. She heads home, armed with new insights into Kenny's mysterious companion.

Mom followed her usual ritual: "Yesterday was such a beautiful school day, wasn't it, Kenny? Did you meet any schoolgirls?" Kenny had a feeling that her questions, like the last time, were leading somewhere. He pondered the question before replying, "Nope."

Mom wondered if she had misspoken again. Maybe that girl wasn't a schoolgirl, and Kenny wasn't lying this time. Deciding there was no point in pursuing it further, she resolved to get to the bottom of it somehow. The next day, at the same time and place, Mom was determined to solve the puzzle. Instead of waiting, she approached the area and found a student loitering nearby. She asked him if he knew about or had seen a red convertible—a hard-to-miss type of car—in the area picking up a student.

"Sure do," the student replied. "She's a prostitute. Beautiful, fancy car—hard to miss. She's been coming here several times lately, though she didn't before. She picks up only one guy from the gang and leaves, probably to the brothel. It makes sense: fancy car, blonde, dark glasses. She's stunning."

Mom's face was a mix of shock and disbelief. She trembled slightly and murmured to herself, "Oh God, not my Kenny."

At home, Mom's thoughts swirled. She couldn't ask Kenny directly, as he would know she had been spying on him and expose her. She wondered if she should use her maternal instincts to avoid playing word games with him again. Mom decided to wait and see if it happened again, as she knew the woman didn't come every day. Mothers are often patient and determined.

Inevitably, the red convertible arrived on schedule: blonde, dark glasses, smiling woman behind the wheel. Kenny eagerly boarded the car. As soon as Mom saw the red convertible approaching Kenny, she rushed to the area. By then, Kenny was already in the car, smiling at Patey.

"Uh-oh, Patey," Kenny said, "my mom's coming. Be careful."

"Stop right there, you whore!" Mom shouted. "How dare you come to a school area to ply your business! Get out of here! What are you doing with my son? Don't you ever come here again. Kenny, get out of this woman's car. I'll deal with you later. For now, go with the gang."

A crowd of students and even some parents watched and listened as Mom unleashed her fury. Patey simply smiled and waited for Kenny to exit the car, not wanting to drive off with Mom yelling at her. Eventually, she slowly pulled away without saying a word.

Oddly, Mom never confronted Kenny about Patey. She assumed he was embarrassed enough not to repeat his actions and that Patey had learned her lesson. However, Kenny and Patey had no intention of stopping their relationship. Kenny knew he would need to be more discreet, and Patey didn't need to pick him up at school anymore.

Kenny tried to apologize to Patey for his mom's tirade and harsh words, but Patey immediately shut him down. "There's no need to apologize," Patey said. "All mothers react like that. I'd think badly of her if she didn't care. She loves you and is trying to protect you,

The French Graduate

that's all. It doesn't bother me at all. My mother would do the same thing. I'll love your mother with you. Please don't blame her. But let's play it safe and not upset her again." Kenny wondered about Patey's perspective and her philosophical take on his mom.

Friday seemed to sneak up on the week like an undercover agent, and many people couldn't wait for it to pass so that Saturday would arrive sooner. As much as Kenny looked forward to the end of the week and Patey's day on Saturday, he felt a bit rushed. It seemed like even the week was eager for Patey. Kenny found it hard to believe that five days had already come and gone; this was his fourth-week meeting with Patey—four times already. Kenny reflected on the progression of their relationship: first, a peck on the cheek, then a closed-mouth kiss, followed by an open-mouth kiss, and finally, a French kiss. This was going to be his fifth week. He wondered what would come next. Little did he know, Patey had a list of events for him and crossed them off one by one. Her plan was working like a charm.

Saturday arrived on time, as it should. The only change was the breakfast menu: hash and scrambled eggs. Kenny was off with the gang early, with no instructions from Mom or Dad, not even a query about his girlfriend. Ben was especially eager to pick up Kenny, Allen, and Glen. The plan was to cruise for girls, even though Kenny wasn't particularly interested. Whenever they could, they pressed Kenny for his thoughts on what Patey might do next and how good his French was. Would he score this time? It was all speculation.

"What if we get some pizza first and then continue with Patey?" Ben suggested.

"That's a brilliant idea," Kenny said. "Why didn't I think of that to stop the twenty questions? I'm not hungry, so I'll just have a slice. I'll be back after going to the flower shop to get Patey a rose."

Kenny went to the flower shop and chose a beautiful red rose. A dozen roses would be impractical to handle. He called Patey to let her know he would be arriving soon. Returning to the gang, he discussed the Patey affair to pass the time while they debated their plans.

After the debate ended, Kenny's eagerly awaited date time arrived. Ben dropped Kenny off at the curb with a rose in hand, just as before. Each of them gave Kenny a fist bump for luck. As Kenny walked up the stairs, he held the rose behind him to keep it hidden. He was about to knock when the door opened, his hand still in the air.

Patey stood at the door as Kenny extended the rose. Her eyes widened in surprise. "Oh, Kenny, that's so sweet of you. Come here," she said. As Patey took the rose and inhaled its fragrance, she embraced him and planted a sensuous kiss on his lips, moaning softly in enjoyment. Kenny soaked in the emotions of the moment, glowing from the lingering kiss that stirred something deep within him. His mind raced with the thought: if one rose could have this effect, what would a dozen do? It was worth every penny.

As Patey pulled back from the kiss and led him to the table, she purred, "You're precious. Not many have brought me flowers for a long time, and that's why I love you. I'll preserve this somehow."

"No, you don't have to," Kenny replied. "I'll bring you a rose of a different color every time I come."

"It's a nice thought, Kenny, but there aren't enough colors to keep up with your wish."

"I hope there are hundreds, and if they run out, I'll pollinate for new ones," Kenny quipped.

"Better cool off with your chilled ale," Patey said, noticing he looked flushed. "Cool down. But I can't get over the precious moment of the rose. It took my breath away, and yet, it's typical of you—insightful. Thank you so much. When you're ready, could you tell me a little about your gang? You don't need to go into detail. I most likely will never meet them anyway. Unless you don't want to go there."

The French Graduate

"No, I don't mind. They're good friends I've had for years, and as you must know, all virgins like me. Their one weakness is girls. Ben's our leader; he has a car and drives us everywhere. We all chip in for gas. He's smart in many ways. Next is Allen, a dependable, mechanically-minded guy. Then comes Glen, a shy but jokey and storytelling type. Just don't get him mad. He helps with anything. They're smart but, like I've been, ambivalent and girl-hungry. We've got each other's backs. And that's it. However, I suspect they're jealous and envious of my seeing and meeting with you. You're the difference in my life. You're my main event. I'd be nothing without you."

Kenny's voice faded as he added, "So, enter the rose—a very small gesture of you on my mind."

"You're saying a lot of things, Kenny—emotional things that I also feel for you too. But I need to end your story for now. I need to manage the time to get you back home and not worry, Mom, okay? Are you ready? I'll do my part; you do yours."

Patey dives onto the bed, crawling on her knees toward Kenny. As he approaches, she unties her robe sash, revealing her boobs, still in her bra. "What have you got for me?" she asks in a sensuous, teasing voice.

Kenny, fully clothed, eyes fixated on Patey's boobs, feels overwhelmed. "What has my French lover got for me?" Patey purrs.

Kenny puts both hands on the bed in front of the hanging boobs, leans forward, clears his throat, and stammers in French. When he finishes, he searches Patey's eyes for her reaction. Is it a yes or no? If it's a yes, what should he do? Should he just follow her lead? Should he take off his clothes? Will she take hers off? Damn, I'm so clueless. All these thoughts are fleeting.

Patey sits back up in bed, still fully exposed, and looks disappointed. She says half-heartedly, "Not good enough. Sorry, but it seems you were distracted by my tits. You need to concentrate and be more intense." She had to say something to address his frustration and not dissuade his efforts to continue his French.

Patey finds it harder each time to refuse Kenny's French, which is getting pretty good, she must admit. But the plan is the plan. Kenny sits at the edge of the bed, facing away from Patey, with a disappointed look—his shoulders drooping, hands on his lap, head hanging down.

Patey crawls over to him, places her boobs on his back, covers his shoulders with her robe, and drapes her arms around him in a consolatory manner, sobbing, "Don't be disappointed, Kenny. You actually did very well under the stress. Maybe I shouldn't have revealed too much; you were blindsided, and this is all new to you. But don't fret; I will teach you the ropes. You'll be amazing, trust me. I'll be your muse. How did it feel with my boobs on your back? Did you feel my body heat? Next time might be braless; would you want that?"

Patey didn't have to ask; she could see his excitement. All this is new to Kenny—from no girls to all women, from a pizza to a nine-course meal, from a river to an ocean.

One small step for Kenny. He was so glad it was with Patey, taking things slowly in baby steps. They each tried to console each other, with Patey being well aware of what she was doing and feeling a tinge of attachment. Patey said, "Well, that had a good outcome. We both won in a way. You're happy with the results, and that's the main thing. Kenny, you handled it the best you could. What I did extra for you is my way of thanking you for the rose. It was precious to me. Sniff time is precious, too."

Patey gave Kenny his marching orders and got up with a smile as if all was well. He was sufficiently satisfied. But before he opened the door, with Patey following her robe still open, Patey pulled him around, pressed her body against his, and French kissed him. "This is my farewell to you, my friend. Hope to see you again," she said with a reassuring grin.

The French Graduate

It's hard to describe Kenny's gait as he floated home. He wondered if Mom would be waiting for him but discounted it, as she usually didn't. So, he returned to reality and normalcy.

Kenny woke up with excited energy. He couldn't wait to see the gang and Mr. Woods. Time seemed to crawl for him. Needless to say, he rushed through breakfast, whatever it was, mumbled a quick goodbye, and was soon on his way with Ben.

"Hey, bud, let's go pick up the others so they can tune in too. It was a doozy. Wait until I give you all the details," Kenny said excitedly.

"It worked. You had sex with her?" Ben responded.

"Ah, no, it didn't go that far, but let me tell you all the details when everyone is here," Kenny said. He didn't mind the wait, but Ben's impatience made him speed up a little. Kenny had to ask him to slow down and be a bit patient. "We've got all week, you know," Kenny confided.

Allen and Glen joined eagerly, and Kenny always sat in the front seat. They all buckled up, with Kenny tugging at his seatbelt to give himself more flexibility to turn and talk to the others in the back seat. He decided to have Ben park at the school lot since they were so early for classes. More waiting was making Ben show some frustration.

"Here we are. Now settle down," Kenny gestured. "You know I bought Patey a red rose? That was a very good move. I held it behind me, and when Patey opened the door, I gave it to her and said something like, 'Babe, for you.' She loved it so much. She spread her arms and pulled me in, planting a kiss of a lifetime—a French kiss, lingering and moaning a little. It was very sensuous and delicious. She gently led me to our ale table again. You guys should try it, chilled ale. Guess what? We talked about you all."

Of all things, she was interested in our gang—just the basics, nothing in detail. When Patey was in the mood for the French proposition, she dove onto the bed, on her knees facing me at the edge of the bed. She untied her robe sash and leaned over to me with her boobs in her bra hanging like fruit in plain view. She waited for my French spiel. I put my hands on the bed, stared directly at her boobs, tried my best under that pressure, and I failed again. Patey straightened up on her knees, showing me disappointment, and so was I.

But when I sat down at the edge of the bed, seeing her disappointed eyes, she crawled over to me, placed her tits on my back, and spread her robe over my shoulders to comfort me, her robe wide open. What a sight and feeling. She sat next to me, and we snuggled together for a while. When it was time for me to leave, I was already high, and it went even higher when she said that next time it would be braless. Then, at the door, I turned to say goodbye, and she French kissed me again. Wow, wow, wow. I floated home; I was in heaven for sure. I couldn't believe this was happening to me. Patey is indescribably beautiful—beyond beautiful.

The gang never once interrupted and devoured every episodic word. It seemed the gang was salivating each time I mentioned boobs or tits and was entranced for half an hour. The bell rang to signal the start of classes, and the gang seemed satiated with the account of my weekly adventure. Next on my agenda was Mr. Woods. When that time came, I related the whole salacious bit. He thanked me for the update but, after hearing about my French rejection again, still believed that intelligent Patey was mentoring me and hiding it from him, using sex as bait. Only time will tell, he concluded. Who am I to burst his bubble? It sure as hell is interesting—a good chess game of strategy. But one thing's for sure: my grades are skyrocketing, and my whole demeanor has changed. One person who noticed was Britta, who always had a liking for me.

It was bound to happen. My gang was getting frustrated that only I had a friend with benefits, leaving everything second-hand for them. Under these circumstances, it was almost inevitable that their frustration with their sexless lives would come to a head. They didn't just want to hear about feelings; they wanted to experience those feelings themselves. Ben conspired with Allen and Glen, minus me, to beef up their zero sex life. But the brothel was out, and they'd never had the guts to talk to girls. They didn't know any girls wanting to hook up with guys, and they certainly didn't speak French. The only girl they knew was Britta, but she was only interested in me. It seemed like I got everything.

The gang had only themselves to blame for their teasing and disrespect, and now it was coming back to bite them. Ben finally concluded, "You know, it narrows down to the only girl we know. It's plain logic, right?" They all looked at each other, considering the prospect. It seemed like a settled plot to make Britta their entry piece.

They discussed the plan. "How on earth are we going to pull this off? We can't just ask her for sex, and we can't ask Kenny for advice about Britta. Let's figure this out ourselves, you know, use our brilliant minds. Why don't we invite Britta to a fake party? We could tell her that Kenny will be there and wants her to come. That might work because she does like Kenny. We'll host it at the Barn House; she's been there before. We'll invite her at the last minute, so she can't make other plans. If she doesn't come, she doesn't come. We're back to square one, still nothing. But if she does come, we'll have to play it by ear. First, we'll ask; if not, beg. If that doesn't work, we might have to resort to some more drastic measures."

Glen asked, "What would that entail?"

"Who knows? This is play-it-by-ear, right?" Ben replied.

They continued planning. "When should we do this? A holiday? Saturday? No, Kenny will be with Patey," they pondered. More questions with no answers were leading nowhere. "Come on, guys, brainstorm."

Glen said, "The conclusion is that we're not clairvoyant; it's unpredictable. We just have to put it in motion to find out. I'm in. I'm starving, if you know what I mean. Sex or die," Glen exclaimed with a wild gesture. They all laughed at the dramatics.

"I'm with Glen. I'm in," agreed another member, while Ben, the original plotter, had a blank stare. "Done deal then. Let's put it in overdrive."

Allen said, "I saw something just posted on the bulletin board about a teachers' conference this Friday, so it'll be a three-day holiday this week. Why not then?"

"Perfect," Ben agreed. "It gives us enough time to set it up. The Barn is free that day. We just need to set up some tables and chairs, some food and drinks, and a cake in a box for the show. Display a few things, and we'll have a party. Easy enough to make two invitations: one for Britta and one for Kenny. Time: 6:30 p.m. Don't tell Kenny anything until he gets there. We'll have to convince him it's for us. He doesn't need sex as much as we do. He must understand that we need excitement, too, not just him. Make sure you have condoms; we can't afford paternity payments."

They all laughed in agreement. That was settled.

The plan proceeded, each one following their assigned tasks. Nothing was said to Kenny during their meetings, just small talk. Kenny mentioned to the gang about the teachers' conference and the free day, noting he had no specific plans, maybe Patey, but most likely not. "What are you guys going to do? Want to go somewhere special?" he asked. Ben only replied vaguely, "Nothing for now, but maybe we'll think of something. Maybe even a party. You never can tell. It's a good opportunity for the three-day holiday," he joked, keeping Kenny in the dark. They spotted Britta talking with her friends, and she stood out to the gang like the main attraction for their planned event, though to Kenny, she seemed no different.

The French Graduate

At the end of the school day on Thursday, Allen asked a friend to deliver an envelope to Britta—the late invitation. Britta was a little surprised, but when she saw that Kenny would be there, she didn't mind. She had just bought a new dress and might wear it to impress Kenny—how lucky she thought. Any concerns about how many of her friends had received invitations or what the party was for quickly faded. "Of course, I'll go," she decided. She needed to tell her mom and dad about the party, and her mom would drop her off. She hoped to be home by 10, but maybe Kenny would bring her home, which would be nice. Maybe they'd dance too, she dreamily thought, adding it to her wish list. "Maybe this will be my lucky night," she mused, though Kenny didn't seem to be into her. She wondered if he had someone else. "Ugh, I'd kill her," she joked to herself, plotting a far-fetched murder-suicide scenario. "What could go wrong?" she pondered, shaking herself out of the fantasy. "Oh yeah, Murphy's Law. Okay, I'll plead insanity. What was I thinking? Thinking is dangerous," she concluded.

Friday arrived, neither too soon nor too late. Everyone seemed excited for the holiday. Plans made on the spur of the moment ruled the day. Everything was flexible. The parents were not affected, but the school kids were. It was time for fun. Since Kenny hadn't decided on what to do, Allen and Glen had their agenda. Ben stopped by Kenny's house early to leave his invitation on the front porch and then drove off. The envelope was addressed only to Kenny, with the details inside: time, 6:30 p.m., and place, Barn House. Kenny thought he heard Ben's car and wondered if he should drop it off himself. "I thought I overheard them mention a party, but I'm not sure," he thought. "I won't call; I'll just see how it goes. I should be done with what Mom has for me. A little late won't matter. I don't think I need to bring anything, not knowing what kind of party it is or what it's for. Bringing myself is good enough. They'd better have plenty to eat. I told Mom not to make anything for me because I was going to a party on the spur of the moment. Just for the food, and I should be home by 10, but don't worry if it's later, depending on the event. Most likely, it's nothing big. An unknown surprise, I suppose."

As Kenny did his chores for his mom, Britta was also helping her mom with housework and odd jobs since there was no school. She was aware of the 6:30 party she had told her mom about and was excited to wear her new dress. Britta had only menial tasks left to do and spent her time casually listening to music and occasionally glancing at the TV. By 6:00, she was all decked out in her new yellow dress, with minor adjustments made by her mom and small talk about what the party might have and that Kenny would be there.

"Do you have his number?" Her mom asked.

"Yes, a friend gave it to me, but I've never called him. I don't think he has mine. We're not that close yet. I kind of like him, but he's always with his gang. He's nice-looking, always laughing and smiling," Britta said.

"The Cannons are a nice family. I've seen Sylvia Cannon a few times around town and talked a little, but I don't know his dad well. They have a nice house, but you know that already," Mom replied.

"Stop it, Mom. Don't speculate, please. Kenny seems clueless about girls, including me. When you're ready, just drop me off outside. I want to look for my friends, okay?" said Britta.

Meanwhile, Kenny's project was taking longer than expected, so he would be late to the beginning of the party. Like Britta's mom, Kenny's mom asked the same type of questions about Britta—typical moms with speculative minds. She reminded Kenny to check the gas, but she thought there was enough. The Barn House wasn't too far, so he left.

At 6:20, Britta urged her mom to get going. "I don't want to be late, and I'm hoping Kenny will be there."

"Kenny, Kenny, isn't that all you can think about? Get your head straight. Then let's head to the Barn House. Mission underway." Her mom replied.

The French Graduate

"Roger that," Britta replied, (thinking, *I hope Kenny's already there and the party is as fun as I expect.*)

At 6:30 sharp, Britta's mom pulled up to the Barn House. Britta stepped out of the car and said, "Looks like I'm early. I can't see Kenny's car from here; they usually park to the side. I'll call you if Kenny brings me home." She bid her mom farewell and walked toward the entrance. Her mom waved goodbye as she drove off.

Britta approached the entrance but couldn't help looking at the parking lot. Only Ben's car was there, which struck her as odd. "Where is everybody?" she wondered. Feeling a little uneasy, she entered the Barn House and noticed there was no greeting party—strange. As she looked around, she saw only the gang whispering to each other. Glen gave her a weak wave and said, "Hi, Britta. You're really early. Want something to drink?"

With only a cooler under the table and a cake box on top, Britta noticed the lack of options. "A soda will do," she said, not specifying a brand. Glen handed her a Coke, and she turned to find a table and seat. "Where is all the food, the beverages, the people? Where is everybody?" she wondered.

Something's wrong. "Is Kenny here?" Britta yells out to the gang.

"No, not yet, but he's coming. Don't worry. More people will be coming soon. Just sit tight."

That odd feeling returns. Here she is, alone with one drink in hand, and no one seems to be coming. Only the gang has been talking among themselves since she arrived. A chill runs down her spine, and her calm demeanor is replaced by a flushed look of panic. Nervously, she gets up and approaches the gang, whom she barely knows personally.

"Hey, something's wrong here. Where is everybody? Where's Kenny? Where's all the food, drinks, music, and games? Or is this all a game? Why am I the only one here? Are you guys trying to trick me? Is this a trap? Have you lost your mind? Wait till I see Kenny!"

Britta's voice rises in volume. Ben speaks up, apologizing to Britta and asking her to calm down and listen.

"Please, Britta, try to understand us. We're not good with girls. We're all virgins, except maybe Kenny, but we want sex from you if possible. We can compensate you, if you're interested, as much as $250."

That was the last straw. "You want to pay me for sex? You think I'm a whore? You can take your money and shove it up your ass. I'm not for sale, you assholes. I'm out of here!" Britta exclaims.

Britta's outburst gets their ire up, and they block her exit. "Well, if these assholes aren't going to get it willingly, these assholes are going to take it," one of them sneers. The three surround Britta, grabbing at her and making her spin around to protect herself. One of them grabs the dress at her shoulder and pulls at it until it tears in half. As Britta tries to cover up, they rip the other half off. The bottom of the dress falls to the floor. Britta instantly covers her panty area, but someone grabs her bra and yanks it off completely. All that's left is her panties.

Half-naked, with her boobs bouncing around as she tries to cover them, a hand grabs the top of Britta's panties, trying to tear them off. Fortunately, they miss and only stretch and tear them a little as Britta sobs and screams. By this time, the gang is pumped up with adrenaline, feasting their eyes on a half-naked woman. It's a first for them.

As fate would have it, Kenny, arriving late, heard the commotion from outside, muffled by the closed door. He wondered why the door was closed for a party. When he opened it, he was confronted with a scene that felt like it was out of a nightmare: his gang was attempting to rape Britta, who was naked and exposed.

"Oh crap, hey, hey, hey!" Kenny shouted at them. "Stop, you idiots! You can't do this. This is trouble for you guys. This is madness. Whatever possessed you, this is definitely, definitely not right. You're hurting her. Can't you see this is not the way to do things? No way! Get away from her!"

Their sensibilities must have returned, as they looked ashamed of what they were doing. They watched as Kenny took off his jacket to cover Britta's half-naked body, barely covering her torn panties.

"You guys clean this place up and go home. I'll handle this," Kenny said as he took Britta to his car and helped her into the passenger seat. She tightly wrapped the jacket around herself. As he started the car and began to drive away slowly, Kenny somberly said, "I'm so sorry about what happened in there. I can't believe or explain what came over them. They're good guys and my friends."

"I don't care. Take me to the station. I'm going to file a report about what happened to me. They need to get what they deserve. They should be held accountable," Britta said firmly.

"Britta, why don't you calm down and let's think about this a little? Don't act too quickly. Let's be rational. I know it's easy for me to say, but you weren't badly hurt—most of the damage was to your clothes, and you're only slightly bruised. Don't make a bigger case out of this. Think about the school, your parents, the publicity, the embarrassment, the media, the negative people, and the rumors among your classmates. There are a lot of negatives involved. Putting these sex-starved guys in prison is not a good choice. Please, Britta, don't do this."

As Kenny drove and pleaded, Britta began to cool down a bit. She listened to his reasoning and agreed that pursuing legal action would cause a lot of grief for everyone involved. "I can just picture my mom and dad; I don't want that scene," she said. It seemed like the best course of action, but she added, "I can't go home like this. My new yellow dress is torn to bits, and I don't have a bra. How am I going to face my mom? She'll be waiting for me."

Kenny tried to analyze the options, prodding himself to concentrate and calculate. "Britta, where did you buy that dress? Is it new?"

"Yes, I just bought it from Mr. Hoofer's dress shop. It's close by," Britta replied, trying to remember if there were more of the same dresses and sizes available.

Kenny, knowing the dress shop's location, drove swiftly to Mr. Hoofer's store, hoping it was still open. It was now 8 PM, and the shop was supposed to close. "Look, Britta," he said urgently, "he's closing up and turning off the lights. We need to hurry." Kenny tried the knob but found it locked. He knocked on the glass door to get Mr. Hoofer's attention, but Mr. Hoofer, already locking up, waved him off and dropped the "Closed" sign.

Desperate, Kenny tapped on the side glass panel to get Mr. Hoofer's attention. Mr. Hoofer, seeing Kenny's earnest pleading and a hand gesture of desperation, rolled up the sign and peered out in the dim light. Seeing Britta, barely covered and visibly distressed, he hesitated.

Britta, feeling a mix of embarrassment and desperation, reluctantly flashed her breasts. Mr. Hoofer, taken aback but sympathetic, opened the door and let them in, explaining, "I'm doing you a favor. Make it quick, find what you need, and leave. My wife is waiting for me."

Kenny and Britta rushed to the rack where Britta had initially found her dress. They searched through the yellow dresses, flipping through sizes. "Ugh, I must have bought the last one in my size," Britta said, noting only a smaller size left. "I tried it on before buying mine, but not much. Let's just get it; we don't have many choices." Kenny had the cash, so it was not a problem. Mr. Hoofer quickly bagged the dress, took the money, and ushered them out.

Back in the car, Britta considered changing into the new dress immediately, but Kenny stopped her. "I can take you to my friend's apartment," he offered. Britta was surprised but relieved. "Oh, that would be nice. Otherwise, it'd be a bit embarrassing. I hope they won't mind."

Kenny felt confident Patey would be understanding. He parked and escorted Britta up to Patey's apartment. Unbeknownst to Kenny, Ben had Allen follow them in Ben's car to report back to the gang. Ben was particularly interested in whether they went to the police. Allen's report was that Kenny and Britta had been driving around for a while, stopped several times, visited a dress shop, bought something, and then went to an apartment. Allen suspected it was Patey's place and noted they had been there for over an hour. "Maybe they're having sex," Allen speculated, "but as long as they didn't go to the police, we're in the clear."

As they approached Patey's apartment, Kenny called Patey to ask a favor. "I need to bring a friend over right now. Is that okay?" Patey's response was immediate and welcoming, "Of course, come on up."

Kenny turned to Britta and explained, "This friend is a woman named Patey. She's a very good friend and can handle this. She will take care of you and make you feel better. Trust me, you'll like her immediately. This is not about me or her; it's about you. I'll explain everything later."

When they arrived at the apartment, Kenny asked Britta to wait in the hallway while he spoke to Patey. Patey, dressed in a long, non-revealing robe, greeted him at the door. Kenny gave her a quick rundown of what had happened, and Patey immediately asked Kenny to call Britta, extending a comforting hand.

"Come in," Patey said warmly, leading Britta inside and assuring her that everything would be alright.

Patey, having been informed of the ordeal Britta had faced and recognizing the urgency, took immediate control of the situation. With experience from traveling and handling delicate situations in her line of work, Patey knew exactly what to do. She guided Britta to the bathroom and closed the door behind them for privacy—a gesture Kenny understood and respected. Patey turned on the shower, gently removing Britta's jacket and torn panty while introducing herself and offering soothing words.

"Don't worry," Patey said calmly. "Take a deep breath and get in the shower. Everything will feel better once you're clean."

Britta, initially hesitant, stepped into the shower. Patey's comforting presence made the experience a bit less daunting. After the shower, Britta emerged with a smile, a sign that Patey's reassurances had worked. She was handed a fluffy towel and a hairdryer to dry her hair. Patey had already prepared a robe, white panties, and a matching white bra as she understood that they were both of same size. Kenny, who had been waiting, felt a wave of relief as Patey and Britta emerged looking refreshed.

Patey led Britta to her dressing table. With practiced hands, she worked on covering up any bruises and brushed Britta's hair. While Patey did most of the work, she allowed Britta to style her own hair, apply makeup, and choose her look. Patey asked if anything was missing, and Britta's response was that everything was perfect.

"If you don't mind me joking," Britta said with a light tone, "with this kind of treatment, I'd almost consider getting 'raped' again." Her attempt at humor prompted a brief laugh from Kenny, a sign of her easing tension. "Good one," Patey said, "A little humor can be uplifting."

When it was time for Britta to change into her new dress, Patey, with a smile, asked if Kenny should leave the room. "No," Britta replied, laughing, "He's already seen me half-naked. It doesn't matter now. I actually prefer it."

Once Britta was fully dressed and primped, she turned to Kenny. "How do I look? You didn't see me before the dress was torn off."

"You look beautiful," Kenny said sincerely, "And that yellow dress suits you perfectly, considering everything. But I must admit, I did like the half-naked look too." They both laughed, easing the tension of the situation.

"Alright, time to go," Patey said, always keeping track of the clock. Britta expressed her profound gratitude to Patey. "I can't thank you enough for everything," Britta said, "Kenny said you'd win me over, and you definitely did. I'll never forget this or you."

"I'm sure that you want me to keep the panty and bra," Britta added with a touch of humor, "I'll cherish them always. Maybe later, I'll ask where you got them—they feel so good."

Patey and Britta shared a heartfelt hug. As Britta was leaving, she noticed Patey sneaking a kiss on Kenny's lips. Kenny mouthed a silent "goodbye" and "thanks" to Patey.

With everything set, Britta prepared to head out. Before leaving, she called her mom to let her know she had a ride home with Kenny. The ordeal was far from over, but for now, Britta and Kenny were ready to face the world with renewed resolve.

Although everything seemed to be in order, a deep-seated apprehension lingered. Nothing ever feels perfect in moments like these. Kenny reminded Britta of their pact—not to mention anything about the night's events. Britta nodded, her expression serious.

It didn't take long for them to arrive at Britta's home. As expected, her parents greeted them warmly when they heard Kenny's car pull in.

"Hi, Kenny! Thank you so much for bringing our daughter home. You saved us a trip," Britta's mom said with a smile. "I hope you had a good time."

"It was alright," Kenny replied, trying to keep his voice steady. "Britta made it nicer for me. She's very funny and attractive."

Kenny blushed slightly. "She brightened up the place with her yellow dress. You have a very beautiful daughter."

"Mom, don't take him seriously," Britta interjected with a laugh. "He says things like that even in his sleep."

"You see," Kenny continued, "she's not only beautiful but also humble." He engaged in light conversation, hoping to deflect any suspicion.

Everything seemed to pass muster, even about Britta's torn yellow dress.

"All right then," Kenny said with a smile, "nice seeing you folks. I'll see you at school, Britta." Britta looked back at him and mouthed a sincere thank you as Kenny drove off, feeling a wave of relief. He wasn't concerned about his own parents waiting up for him—he knew sleep would come hard, if at all. Nightmares seemed more likely.

This was not a day Kenny wanted to wake up to. His gang—ugh, his gang—had tried to gang-rape Britta. Good lord, how could this happen? His own classmates, and they'd even invited him. To what? Participate? A fake party, a trap? What was wrong with the world?

The French Graduate

Kenny tossed and turned in bed, grappling with the weight of what had happened. What was he supposed to say to them now? Would this end their friendship or somehow bring them closer? There was today and tomorrow to figure things out. What about Britta? What about Patey—should he see her today? He hoped so. Maybe she could help him make sense of it all. She'd studied philosophy; perhaps she could offer some guidance.

This was not something he could share with Mr. Woods or anyone else. It was something to be buried deep, six feet under. He knew his mom would definitely ask about the party. He hoped that no one else would know. It wasn't advertised, so that was a plus. Britta wouldn't say a word, but did that mean he had to lie about everything?

Breakfast was ready, but Kenny was running late. His mom, noting his disheveled appearance, guessed he must have had a late night. "Good morning, sleepyhead. Came in late?" she asked, her tone tinged with concern.

"Umm, yeah, I just overslept. A little tired, I guess. I'm hungry, though," Kenny replied. The party hadn't had any food, and all the drama had only made things worse. Pancakes were a welcome relief, and hash browns made it even better. He ate in silence, trying to fend off thoughts about the previous night.

"Did you have a good time last night?" his mom asked, breaking the quiet. "Lots of food and dancing? Was Britta there?"

Kenny tensed at the mention of Britta. "Britta? Why are you asking about her?" he replied, trying to sound casual. "Yes, she was there. So?"

"Well, there are some rumors going around that you like her and that you were seen talking to her. Is something going on?" she asked, sounding more curious than accusatory.

Kenny was taken aback. Did she know something? "Uh, no, not really. Just friends," he said, hoping to deflect further questions. "By the way, Mom, do you have any jobs for me today? Nothing big, though—I've got something this afternoon."

Not with the gang, of course; he wasn't telling her about any conflict with them, hoping she wouldn't pry into what he did with the gang. He hoped that Britta was alright and had no flashbacks. Meeting Patey was good for her, and Patey told Britta to call her if she needed more mental clearing. That is her specialty—therapy. Britta has Patey's number. Kenny is confident that Britta is a strong person, level-headed, and tough. A beautiful girl, beautiful mind, beautiful tits, too. He couldn't help looking at them secretly and admiringly; they were just there. It was difficult to erase them from his mind and thoughts, so much so that he didn't remember if Mom had a project for him. He had to ask again. Mom told him not to worry about it and that it wasn't a priority but wanted him to look at it and fix it, provided it was done before 2 o'clock. Not a problem, he told Mom.

At 2 p.m., Kenny was ready to head out, eager to see Patey and get her reaction to the events. He mentioned to his mom that he would take the bike for some exercise and would be back for dinner. "Just be careful," she replied, her concern evident.

On the way, Kenny stopped to call Patey and let her know he was on his way. Upon arriving at her apartment, he found the bike rack, locked his bike, and walked to the door. It was left slightly ajar for him. Patey greeted him with a warm smile as she set up the chilled drinks.

"Sorry I'm a little late," she apologized, beckoning Kenny inside. She leaned in and kissed him on the lips sweetly—a gesture that had become routine between them. Kenny had grown accustomed to these kisses, finding comfort in their familiarity.

"Thanks, Patey," Kenny said, his voice filled with relief. "I really needed that kiss. My mind is all messed up right now. You did

The French Graduate

a wonderful job with Britta. Everything went smoothly with her parents, and even the dress was fine. She can't thank you enough. You've earned a friend for life from her. And I must admit, you are beautiful, which I already knew."

Patey smiled, clearly pleased by Kenny's words. She poured him a drink, and they settled into comfortable conversation. The mood was lighter, and Kenny found solace in Patey's company, hoping that their discussion could help him make sense of the chaos and find a path forward.

The tension from last night still hung in the air.

"Kenny, relax. Breathe. Sit down and cool off with your favorite drink—the ale you love," Patey said, trying to lighten the mood. "I need one too. Let's toast to making it through so far."

Kenny sighed, sinking into a chair. "Patey, I can't even imagine if you hadn't been there. If you weren't an option for us, the gang and I would be sitting in a jail cell right now. It shouldn't have happened, but it did. Thank God you were there."

"That's life, Kenny. Shit happens all the time. You were lucky, though, and it's good you convinced Britta not to report it. You didn't do anything wrong, but you saved a lot of people. Now, it all depends on how your gang moves forward."

Kenny took a deep breath, finally allowing himself to relax. "For now, let's just enjoy this moment. I miss you, you know, even if it was...last night." He chuckled, taking a sip of his ale. "This drink, you, this moment—it's like an elixir. I just want to sit here, drink with you, and say...I love you. Let's let this moment wash over us, calm us like a yoga session. Let's pause and find peace."

Patey smiled. "Wow, Kenny, that was profound. I like this mood. Let's clear our minds and think rationally. You're here to process everything that happened. It's not a big deal—no crime was committed, just some emotional fallout. The question is, will your gang take responsibility for their actions? Will this shake them up, make them rethink their impulses and how they see the world?" Patey's voice turned philosophical.

"The next few days will be crucial," Kenny said, nodding. "I'll have to take the high road. I'm just glad I stood up for Britta, and for you. What I did for Britta, I did for both of you. I hope you see that."

Patey leaned in closer, her eyes softening. "I do, Kenny. And that's why I love you. You're like a hero, you know that? Saving everyone around you."

Kenny laughed, shaking his head. "Yeah, a hero who can't even save himself. Do heroes get extra benefits?"

Patey's smile faded. "Kenny, this isn't the time for jokes. You have a real problem to solve. Your relationship with the gang is shattered. They might blame you or Britta, and they'll probably keep their distance. Be prepared for that. Don't let it rattle you. Just be yourself."

She hesitated before adding, "And keep Britta away from them, if you can. It's her best option. Remember, she might have flashbacks or panic. If she needs someone to talk to, tell her to call me. I can take her out and get her mind off things. A little one-on-one girl time might help."

Kenny nodded. "I'll tell her. She likes you, you know. Seems you've got another admirer."

"You really have a knack with people. Everyone can't help but love you. Charismatic—that's the word for you. Irresistible from day one, and you know it," Kenny said, his tone filled with admiration. "Britta was lucky you were here at the right time. Now, it seems like we've got a bit of a conundrum, you and me. We both want to help

The French Graduate

Britta. She's tough, and I bet she put up a hell of a fight. It's just too bad she was outnumbered—she would've won one-on-one, no doubt."

Patey nodded thoughtfully. "She did incredibly well under the circumstances. As for your gang, I've already told you what to expect. They'll come to their senses and realize how wrong they were. They're lucky to have a friend like you. Just give them a little time. It's only logical, especially since I'm also clairvoyant," she added with a playful giggle. "This will all pass, thanks to one key ingredient—you, my Kenny. You did the mature thing, and maybe it was your DNA kicking in at just the right time. Who knows? Anyway, just take it one day at a time. It will all work out, trust me."

Patey leaned back with a sigh. "Okay, the session's over. Hope the check will be in the mail," she joked, her laughter lightening the mood. "Time waits for no one, Kenny. You'll have to take a raincheck on your pleasure agenda today. No French class for us—sorry for you and sorry for me."

Kenny slouched, feigning disappointment. "I do look forward to our... sessions, those tingling feelings."

Patey replied, "You might get withdrawal pains, but you'll survive. Just don't forget—if Britta needs anything, let me know. Keep me posted on any major stuff, not the small things. Let me process it all."

Patey paused, then added with a grin "But for now, my big, mature man, come here. You kiss me this time. Take the initiative."

There was only a slight hesitation from Kenny, but he felt ready. Approaching a woman and kissing her wasn't something deeply embedded in his memory bank, but he had a great teacher—the best. He rationalized, as Patey often did, that it was a man's role to take the initiative most of the time. She was nudging him to step up to take control of the situation, so he decided to give it his best shot.

He wrapped his arms around her, pulled her closer, and pressed his lips to hers. He felt her lips quiver as he leaned into the kiss, letting it deepen into a French kiss. He thought, *She taught me well.* Her soft moan was all the approval he needed. When he finally pulled away, she smiled, clearly pleased.

"Good job," she murmured, her eyes twinkling. "Now, go home—not as a boy, but as a man."

As Patey had predicted, the gang shunned Kenny like he was an unwelcome guest. They acted as if nothing had happened just days ago. Kenny decided that the ball was in their court—let them make the first move, not him. Patey remained optimistic about the outcome, but the gang was a different story. They started spreading rumors, calling Britta a cock teaser and a slut, claiming she tried to seduce them at a private party last Friday night and ended up taking Kenny to a hotel for sex.

The gang felt safe, thinking neither Kenny nor Britta would mention the party. Both of them kept silent, enduring the stares and whispers from their classmates. Was Patey right that this would all blow over in time? But the rumors didn't die down; they only got worse as the days passed, becoming more blatant and hateful. It was harder on Britta than on Kenny, and she was fed up. She had thought they'd want to bury the incident, not give it more life. *Are they that dumb?*

By Thursday night, Britta had reached her breaking point. She decided that come tomorrow, she would confront them. *Damn it, I'm going to kick their balls in.*

Friday came, the end of the week and the end of her patience. It was inevitable that they would push her to the edge. They had practically begged for this confrontation. Britta, the wild one, saw them gathered together and felt a surge of adrenaline. Her anger ignited, and she marched straight up to the group, fists clenched.

The French Graduate

"Ben, you and your buddies tried to rape me! I'm the victim here, but you assholes don't get it!" she spat, her voice trembling with fury. "You're spreading rumors like it's my fault—and Kenny's. Are you really that fucking clueless? Kenny saved your asses! I could've and wanted to, turn you in to the police for what you did. It's called attempted rape, and it carries a 20-year sentence. You're damn lucky Kenny begged me not to."

Britta's words hit them like a sledgehammer. "The only reason you're not rotting in jail right now is because of Kenny. And now you're out here spreading bullshit rumors? Are you that dumb? Kenny and I are not lovers. He's the one who spent his own money to buy me a new dress from Mr. Hoefer's shop, to replace the one you animals tore off me. If he hadn't done that, my mom would have called the cops in a heartbeat."

She took a step closer, her eyes blazing with anger. "Kenny took me to his girlfriend Patey's house, and she patched me up so I could go home without raising alarms. He protected me, you idiots! You should be ashamed of yourselves. You owe Kenny a damn apology—and not just him. Think about the school and the families involved. Do you have any idea how close you came to causing a disaster?"

Britta's voice dropped to a dangerous whisper. "I could still report it if you don't stop spreading this shit. Fair warning: I'd rather be nice, but it's your choice. Your fucking choice."

Kenny had no idea that Britta had confronted the gang. So, when he found an invitation to another party at the Barn House in his porch, just like before—he was immediately suspicious. The invite was marked *urgent* and read: "Must attend. Saturday, 6 PM. Casual, low budget. Bring food and drink. Dance to taped music. Ends at 9 PM. Everyone invited. Drag a friend. Surprise event."

Kenny couldn't shake his unease. After everything that had happened, why would they want him at another party? But what Kenny didn't know was that the gang had undergone a sort of epiphany after Britta confronted them. Her blunt exposure of their bullshit narrative had cut deep. They realized just how misguided and wrong they were and how much trauma they had caused her. Confronted with the truth, they couldn't deny the damage they had done.

The gang deeply, sincerely apologized to Britta. They were awed by how she handled herself, standing up to them despite everything they'd put her through. It was tough as hell, but she remained level-headed, even giving them a chance to make things right. They knew now that Britta wasn't just some random girl—they were lucky to have her as a friend.

In a gesture of solidarity, the three of them placed their hands together and extended them to Britta as a token of their newfound respect and friendship. They promised to be more mature and respectful to everyone. Britta didn't hesitate—she could see their sincerity. *"Look, guys, it was a bad start, but it doesn't have to stay stuck in neutral. There's a lot of road left to travel in life. You need to make it up to Kenny. You should know that he doesn't have any bad feelings toward you. He still wants to be part of the gang—he loves you guys. He's told me so many times. If you want, I can help you with that."*

It didn't take long for the three of them to come up with a plan. Britta and her friends offered to help organize another party at the Barn House—this time, a real one. On the surface, it would be just a regular party, but the real purpose would be to apologize and honor Kenny, who had emerged as a true friend and outstanding student. The gang realized Kenny had broken out of his shell, becoming something more—a butterfly among them. They agreed it could work if everyone pitched in.

Britta exchanged numbers with Ben to coordinate the details, and they spent the week planning. As Monday rolled around, Kenny's mom noticed something was off. Ben hadn't been picking Kenny up lately, and he was riding his ten-speed to school instead. When she asked about it, Kenny shrugged it off, saying Ben was dealing with some car trouble and that he needed the exercise anyway. He mentioned another party this weekend, but his mom didn't seem too concerned. School seemed back to normal—no sign of the gang and no more harassment or rumors about Britta. A good sign, Kenny thought.

As the days passed, Britta occasionally checked in with Kenny. She reminded him about the party, made it clear that she was definitely going, and told him she needed him for comfort. How could he refuse, knowing everything she had been through?

Kenny knew he'd have to tell Patey about the party during their time together—it was a major development she'd need to digest. "Well, that's a surprise. I didn't see that coming, but it's a good one. And you say Britta is definitely going? That's even better. She's a beautiful and tough woman. It's good to see she's getting over it. Give her my regards. Keep me posted on all the details next time. Love you." Kenny was now fully committed to attending the party, though he was reluctant to rain-check his "pleasure course" with Patey for the second time. That sucked—something he was hesitant to admit.

Asking his mom for the car and getting her to make something to bring to the party was just another step in solidifying his commitment to go, even though part of him still wished he could just be with Patey instead. *I'll be forever wondering what I'm missing,* he thought. He could've made time, but Britta wanted him to pick her up along with the food her mom had made for the party. And, of course, he had to do it in front of her mom and dad—her parents liked him so much, and he needed to bring her home after. Not that he minded; Britta was charming, smart, and funny. *I wonder what she'll be wearing—better not be yellow,* he thought. There were so many things he needed to talk to her about, including Patey. He wondered how she'd take it. He didn't think it would change anything—Britta and Patey really liked each other. But would they get any time alone to engage in these issues? What if the party was crowded? Then what?

With Britta and the back seat full of food, Kenny was hard-pressed to find a parking space. He first drove to the back, where people were waiting to take their food to the table inside, then finally found a spot to park. They both entered the Barn and despite the crowd, finding a table was easy—the gang had reserved one for Britta and Kenny. Someone even escorted them to the table, which Britta had planned herself, unbeknownst to Kenny.

"Hey, Britta, did you notice that? We got special treatment. I don't get it—are you an undercover queen?" Kenny joked. Britta just laughed. "Must've been a mistake, I guess."

Aware of how women might feel in social situations, Kenny asked Britta if she had a drink preference, offering to get her a second choice if they didn't have her first. Kenny was surprised when she simply asked for a ginger ale. He brought back four, saving a trip for refills. They toasted each other as they listened to the low background music, surrounded by people chatting, singing along, and generally enjoying the festive atmosphere while waiting for the buffet to open.

Kenny and Britta didn't rush to eat. They sipped their drinks while Kenny quietly asked Britta how she was handling things with the gang. He mentioned Patey's offer to help in any way she could. Kenny also noticed his gang was there, busy doing chores or something. "Let me know if they try to bother you. There are too many people here for them to pull anything," he assured her.

As the party continued and they finished eating, Kenny, thoroughly enjoying every moment with Britta, was momentarily distracted when a gong sounded for silence and a voice came over the mic. "Your attention, please! This special party was set up by the senior class students, especially the girls, led by Britta Reeves and a handful of senior boys. They deserve all the credit for pulling this off in just one week. But tonight, we're here to honor a special senior—a straight-A student who, unknown to him, has been chosen as our Valedictorian speaker. He's been kept in the dark, so this will be a total surprise. Everyone, please rise for... Mr. Kenny Cannon!" Applause

The French Graduate

erupted, and Kenny, stunned, stood up. He looked at Britta, completely dumbfounded. "You knew about this and set me up?" he asked.

"Yep. We're all proud of you. Can I kiss you for that?" Britta responded with a grin, then leaned in and gave him a quick kiss on the lips. His gang came forward, each of them hugging him and saying things like, "You the man." The room filled with congratulations, and once that was over, the music cranked up, and the dance floor opened. Britta could barely wait for Kenny to ask her to dance. When he finally did, they swayed together to a slow song, their bodies close, making it a night neither of them would forget. Afterward, Kenny drove Britta home to her mom and dad. She gave him a peck on the cheek as a thank-you for the ride, and with a wink, they said goodnight.

The next day didn't wait for Kenny—it arrived right on time, feeling extra bright and inviting. Over breakfast, Kenny told his mom all about the surprise party. "It was all set up by Britta, the gang, and a lot of the community and teachers. The big surprise? They chose me to be the Valedictorian speaker at graduation in May. There was dance music, and yeah, I danced with Britta. She's a special friend, but she's not my girlfriend. Oh, and Ben's car is fixed, so my bike's retired for a while. My muscles are aching, but it's working up my appetite. There was a lot of food, but I mostly ate Britta's mom's roast pork—very tasty. I took Britta home and got a little peck from her, just so you know, in case you need to know."

School days don't arrive timidly—they roar in, like it or not, but life goes on with the usual normalcy. A good breakfast, a good breezy ride, and a school that's there to seduce minds. Kenny was now on a mission: learn the subject to apply it to life. Learn French to seduce a woman—Patey. What once seemed difficult and impossible was now attainable; the impossible just took a little longer, it seemed. French was now manageable and interesting, and interacting with the teacher and classmates made it even more enjoyable. Mr. Woods couldn't be happier—everyone else was just as eager to participate now that Kenny was engaged. And with this kind of atmosphere, any week could fly by with fulfillment.

It was the same old Saturday, and there was no turning back. This was Kenny's day to be with Patey. But now, Kenny was back with his gang, starting fresh. The tension with Britta had eased; she was no longer an issue. As the gang gathered, slipping back into their usual girl-chasing banter, they couldn't resist teasing Kenny about the kiss he got from Britta. They wanted to know if it felt any different from kissing Patey.

Kenny shrugged it off. "It was planets apart. Britta's kiss wasn't passionate; it was just a kiss, no strings attached. I can't wait for you guys to get your first kiss; then you'll understand."

Glen suggested they park at the pizza parlor and scope out some girls. Everyone agreed it was a solid plan. If no girls showed up, at least they'd get something to eat. Kenny didn't care much—he had his mind on other things. They parked, popped in a Taylor Swift CD, and leaned back to enjoy the moment. After a while, they spotted four girls approaching the parlor, chatting and laughing loudly. Their laughter caught the gang's attention, and Ben cranked up the volume as they passed by. The music made the girls pause, searching for the source, and one of them pointed toward the car. The gang wondered if the girls were checking them out or just the car, but it didn't matter—it had gotten their attention.

As the girls went inside to find a table, the gang followed and found a spot with a clear view of them. Glen went to place their order and then returned to wait. The girls, meanwhile, were chatting and laughing while the gang, in contrast, sat quietly, observing them. When the girls' pizza arrived, they started eating politely while the gang dug into theirs with a bit more enthusiasm. But soon enough, they slowed down, trying to stretch out the meal so they could stay longer and watch the girls.

The French Graduate

Eventually, Ben turned to Kenny and asked if he could go over and ask the girls if they wanted company. "I don't have the balls to do it," Ben admitted.

Kenny shook his head. "Not today, man. I've got to get ready for my date with Patey and buy her a rose. But next time, I'll do it. Promise."

He started planning. "Glen, walk past their table and check out what kind of pizza they're eating—discreetly. I want to see how they react."

Glen got up and walked past the girls' table, and Kenny watched their reaction. Did they notice him? Did they nudge each other or giggle? This was Kenny's way of sizing up the situation for when he'd have to make a move. As both groups started showing signs of leaving, Kenny gave the girls a small wave goodbye.

Afterward, Kenny headed to the flower shop and picked out a lavender rose for Patey.

As Ben dropped Kenny off, Kenny smoothed out his clothes and fingered his hair a bit, carefully cradling the delicate rose. He held it out in front of him like a prized possession, ready to present it to Patey. When he reached the doorway, Patey struck a seductive Hollywood pose and murmured, "You come here often," pulling her robe halfway open to reveal her panties and bra. Kenny struggled to keep a straight face, a grin threatening to break through. He extended the rose toward her and asked, grinning, "The rose or a kiss?"

Patey, breaking character, tapped her chin thoughtfully and replied, "I'm thinking, I'm thinking." They both burst into laughter, and Patey pulled Kenny into a warm embrace, followed by a kiss. It was a well-played moment, and they both laughed their way to the awaiting chilled ale.

"Drink and toast first, catch your breath, relax for a bit," Patey advised. After they settled down, she wanted to hear about Kenny's day. "Tell me what you did before you came here."

Kenny shrugged, "Not much. The gang and I were out hunting for girls—well, not for me, for them. We hit up a pizza parlor, had some pizza, and then left. There were four girls there that the gang was all excited about. They wanted me to break the ice with them. I promised I'd do it next time, not today, since I haven't seen you for three weeks. I was having palpitations, ha-ha."

"That was quick," Patey said, raising an eyebrow. "I think you did that on purpose. Three weeks is pushing it, even for me. I miss you badly, so I'll push that envelope for you."

"Three weeks should not be forced on anyone, but it happens, even to the best," Kenny said. "Thanks for the beautiful lavender rose. I love lavender. But, like you pointed out, hybrids are pretty but lack a strong fragrance. It's the thought that counts, though. And that kiss was very good—delicious, even. Are you practicing with Britta? Just kidding."

Kenny confessed, "I have to admit, Britta kissed me at the party to congratulate me for the award I received."

"Excuse me, what award?" Patey asked.

"Oh, I didn't get a chance to tell you. The party last Saturday was a surprise party for me. Britta confronted the gang, kicked their asses, and straightened them out. Now they're so-called new friends. The party was their idea as a way to apologize and clear the air for a fresh start. I didn't know about it beforehand. They celebrated me for getting straight A's and being chosen as the valedictorian speaker at graduation."

"Oh, Kenny, I'm so proud of you. You deserve every bit of it. That's amazing news. Thanks for telling me."

The French Graduate

Patey listened intently, relaxing with her robe open, giving Kenny an eyeful of her panties and bra. Kenny was starting to get used to the sight.

Patey had reviewed her list of sexual encounters with Kenny, and this one was a real standout. "Kenny, before you indulge in your French treat, I've got something extra to spice things up. Listen carefully and follow my instructions exactly—no improvisations, no deviations. Come with me to the bathroom. I'm going to take a shower for your viewing pleasure. Remove my robe and hang it up. Then, take off my bra and panties and place them neatly with the others. Watch me as I shower, and when I'm done, spread a towel for me to step on, and you can dry me off—except for you-know-where. Hand me a second towel so I can dry my [privates] and hair. You can take care of drying my tits. Once I'm dry, I'll put my panties and bra back on but will need you to hook the bra for me. After that, I'll slip back into my robe, and we can return to the bed. You're sharp and observant, so I won't repeat myself." It was almost as if the instructions had been typed out by a robotic assistant and saved in memory. Kenny's crisp salute signaled that everything was locked in. Every pleasure was delivered as planned. Patey then slipped on her robe and guided Kenny back to the bed.

Standing there, as promised, Patey began unbuttoning Kenny's shirt, then slid into a sexy pose, inviting Kenny to seduce her. However, distractions always seemed to cloud his mind, preventing him from fully engaging in his 'French' skills. Despite his advanced techniques, the gang, the party, and the overwhelming allure of the moment made it impossible. Kenny knew his efforts would be futile. His French was barely hanging on, practically lifeless. Sitting down on the bed, Kenny shook his head in frustration. Patey saw that he was completely drained, despite her efforts to entice him. He looked utterly dejected. Crawling over to him, she gently lifted her bra, resting her warm breasts on his back, holding him close. Kenny could feel the heat from her chest and the softness of her breasts against him. How could anyone not respond to that? There was no deleting this moment—it was all saved. Although he didn't succeed, it wasn't a total loss. Even the simple kiss goodbye felt like a small victory.

Back to normalcy isn't easy, a tug and pull is normal.

The adulation for their discontent had ended; now it was back to the daily grind. Time moves quickly when the work is rewarding. Classes and French are becoming more manageable, but perfection is still out of reach. The gang was captivated by Kenny's unembellished tales of his encounters with Patey. Mr. Woods also enjoyed his share of Patey's perks, enough to make any virgin envious. Yet, Mr. Woods noticed Kenny's French was still lacking, deepening his suspicions about a mentorship. His wife shares these suspicions.

Patey is fully aware that Kenny shares what he has done with Patey with others. She doesn't mind the exposure, always mindful of how she's guiding Kenny through sexual matters with subtle yet sensuous escapades. Patey knows she must keep the momentum alive. There's never any doubt in her mind about her actions—it's a virtual experience for Kenny and a vicarious thrill for everyone else.

Kenny hoped there wouldn't be any unexpected drama—at least not until next week, he mused. Classes had become more enjoyable; French was no longer unbearable but rather inspiring and even desirable. The gang was still together, his grades were improving, and he had more friends than ever. And then there was Britta, who seemed to be showing some interest in him. He felt a slight, confusing attraction toward her, unsure of how to interpret these new feelings. Was it possible...? He stopped himself from thinking further. "Keep that thought," he told himself. However, thoughts have a way of becoming reality, and Britta cornered Kenny during a break. Britta was known for being direct—case in point, her bold confrontation with the gang. Without hesitation, Britta asked, "Kenny, can I ask you a personal question?" "Go ahead, we're supposed to be friends now, right?" Kenny replied. "Not just supposed to be—we are friends now," Britta confirmed, then continued, "Is Patey your girlfriend? She's a bit

The French Graduate

older than you but still looks young and beautiful. I saw you kiss her when we left. She's so full of life, and you do know French..."

"Funny you mention French. Patey was born in France. She's fluent—better than my French teacher. She can handle almost anything. She studied psychiatry and psychology at a French university. She's the reason I have an 'A' in French now instead of an 'F'," Kenny confided. "Oh, now I get it—your transformation must have started when you met her. I've been watching you in class for a while, but you never noticed me. I'm the low-key type, like my mom," Britta revealed. "I have to admit, I never noticed. I was clueless before, but not anymore. Patey's taught me a lot—more than you'd believe. You'd be shocked if I told you...really shocked. But I don't think I can share it. It's very personal. I've told guys about it, and from that, you can read between the lines—it's a sexual thing, so you can see why it's hard to discuss with you, even though we're friends," Kenny explained.

Britta then asked, "Do you love her? It's a simple question, something I need to know. I can't ask if she loves you—I'd have to ask her that." Kenny realized Britta had only met Patey once and knew only what he had told her. He decided Britta should learn more, sooner rather than later. "Britta, this may shock you and might be hard to understand, but I hope it doesn't change anything between us. It may not be what you think—Patey is a prostitute. I met her at a brothel we found."

In spite of what you're thinking right now, we've never had sex so far. I can't quite explain it; it's complicated. We've been together for months, so why no sex? After all, it's her forte. How can I put this into words? I can't. I can't help but love her; she is truly one of a kind and magnificent. She's beautiful, sexy, sensual, and seductive. It's impossible not to love her. But is this real love? I don't know, and I can't say whether it is. I want to understand what love is; can you tell me what it is, Britta? Kenny asked soulfully. "I don't know either; I'm still searching too. If Patey is a prostitute, she's the best in my book.

She helped me instantly, without hesitation, and gave me underclothes that I will cherish—they're the best I've ever had. I can't blame you for loving her, but do you love her for what she signifies, a Near-Goddess? Britta confided. "There's a lot of truth in what you say. I'm fascinated by her every move, and in a way, she gives me sexual treats that I'm too embarrassed to share with you. But I must admit, I've learned a lot about women and sex, but in a respectful and perceptive way. That's also why I saved you. Patey was my muse. She inspired me to be respectful to everyone. Is that her philosophy, or is it in her DNA like mine? What about you, Britta? A Wonder Woman in your past, beautiful and strong?" Kenny queried. "I don't really know; maybe my mom is intelligent. I hope some of that rubs off on me," Britta said with a hopeful tone. I find it hard to accept the no-sex answer, but from what you've just hinted at, I'm trusting you to be honest about it. However, you've given me the impression that you wish it had happened, so it feels believable. I secretly hope it didn't. Let that linger in your thoughts," Britta responded. "Well, thank you for your honesty and concern. Life is complex; love is even more so. To be honest, I'm a little attracted to you—not just because I saw you half-naked. There's something about you that pulls my interest, and I do want us to be best friends. I love Patey, and she seems to love me. We share each other for now. But deep down inside, I have doubts about myself and Patey. I feel insufficient, not in her league—DNA included. With that in mind, let's stay good friends with no cords attached. But don't let me hold you back if something comes along for you, okay?" Kenny said with a heavy moan. Britta leaned in to Kenny, kissed him on the cheek, and said, "I'm in." Then she headed off to class. Kenny touched where Britta kissed him and smiled.

In French class, Kenny would always speak in French instead of English, which motivated the rest of the class to respond in the same way. Mr. Woods enjoyed the lively repartee and would eagerly contribute to the conversation. Suddenly, French became fun.

When the French class was over, Mr. Woods thanked Kenny for stirring up the class and making it enjoyable for everyone else, too.

The French Graduate

Then, with a quizzical look, he asked Kenny why he flunked out again. "You say you had a crisis to distract from a party, but you're having a dry spell on your approval rating, aren't you?" he said, relating to Kenny. Mr. Woods knew full well that Patey was just baiting him with her sex angle. But he realized he would be a fool to expose that to Kenny. He figured that Kenny was smart enough to figure it out someday—just not from him. Kenny is a rare person who comes along only rarely; he is truly a gift.

The need for the school week to end is palpable among everyone connected to Kenny. The gang is eagerly anticipating the girls at the pizza parlor and Kenny's promise to perform for them. Kenny is almost certain they will show up, judging by their reactions to Glen and the gang. So, the gang is pumped to head to the pizza parlor and wait once more at the same spot for those four girls to cross paths again. Waiting often feels futile until it pays off. The same girls approach, but this time they pass by even closer, laughing louder than before, perhaps to draw attention. While they waited, Kenny shared his plan with Glen: when the girls place their order, see if they order the same thing as last time. "Okay, there they go. Wait about five minutes, then we'll go in. You can place our order while I talk to the manager. Just sit tight." The girls got their orders and started eating and chatting, glancing at the gang now and then. When Glen returned with their order and an extra pizza, Kenny picked up the additional pizza and walked over to the girls. He introduced himself, confessing that he had brought a large pizza for them, joking about adding weight, which made them laugh. He asked if they minded his gang joining them, presenting the pizza as an offering. "If it's okay, I've asked the manager to set up a connecting table and chairs. Let me introduce everyone: I'm Kenny, and there are Ben, Allen, and Glen, whom you've seen pass by many times. Just a heads-up: they're shy around girls; you're their first, so be gentle," he said with a chuckle. The girls straightened up and giggled at this. The manager picked up on the vibe and quickly set up a table and chairs for everyone.

Kenny waved to the gang, signaling them to come over, and they saw the tables being joined, approaching sheepishly.

Standing, each person introduced themselves before taking a seat until all three were settled. The gang eagerly opened their boxes, retrieving their slices of pizza, with Kenny reminding them to be polite and respectful as they ate. Naturally, they hit it off wonderfully. Glen was in his element, cracking joke after joke that had everyone in stitches. Alongside the laughter, they engaged in deeper conversations that genuinely intrigued the girls. The gathering wrapped up on a high note, with both sides expressing their desire to meet again, setting a date to return to this spot. The gang couldn't hide their excitement and newfound belief; they felt like they were glowing in the dark and couldn't thank Kenny enough for facilitating the get-together. Kenny himself felt a swell of pride.

As the familiar routine of the week unfolded, days drifted by like summer rain. Britta continued her playful flirting with Kenny, while the gang buzzed with excitement from their latest adventure. Mom and Dad remained on an emotional rollercoaster, and French was still waiting in the wings. Saturday had arrived, and Swedish pancakes were the breakfast of choice from Kenny. He felt he deserved this treat, and indeed, it brightened anyone's day. Ben eagerly pulled into the driveway and waited patiently, mindful not to beep his horn in rudeness. Being anxiously early was not anyone's fault in particular. This was Saturday, not a school day, yet they all wanted Kenny there to introduce them to their new girlfriends; one day wouldn't give them the confidence they needed. They were still apprehensive around girls and needed Kenny like a comforting security blanket. This was no problem for Kenny; he enjoyed chatting with girls, especially Britta and Patey.

So Kenny emerged whistling a cheerful tune with a lighthearted shuffle. "Hey, bud! You seem to be in a great mood. Hmmm, nice shirt and a lovely smile—nothing beats optimism, I say. Maybe you'll get as lucky as I did with Patey," he beamed. Both in

The French Graduate

high spirits, they cranked up the volume as they headed out to pick up Allen and Glen for their pizza rendezvous with the girls. They waited outside for a little while to pass the time, chatting about the girls—guy talk, like who was cute, funny, or shy, and other stuff like that. By 11:00, they headed inside, with Kenny getting the manager's approval to push the tables together; after all, it was good for business. The wait was brief, and soon, the four pizza girls arrived. The girls insisted that everyone should pay for their own orders. Kenny agreed on behalf of the group; it certainly wasn't a deal breaker and was a reasonable arrangement. As usual, Glen had a fresh batch of jokes and anecdotes ready. It turned into a great session filled with laughter, teasing, conversations, revelations, and confessions. They wrapped up by exchanging phone numbers and confirming a definite next meet-up for the following week. Kenny was straightforward about his relationship status, explaining that he might not always be available, which limited his interactions with them.

As the gang waved goodbye to the girls, Kenny called out to Patey, then decided to buy a bright yellow rose. The gang, in high spirits, dropped Kenny off at Patey's place. He didn't try to hide the rose; instead, it became part of his signature look whenever he visited her. Patey stood at the door, waiting and watching as Kenny approached. He wrapped her in a tight hug, lifting her slightly to kiss her passionately before carrying her to the table. "Hmm, that was delicious and bold. I like it. Good move! I've got a good supply of chilled ale, so we can chat comfortably." Patey had many insights about life and philosophy that hadn't been mentioned before. Each time Kenny visited, she shared stories about her life in France, her travels, and the solutions she found to various obstacles. Then they shifted the conversation to Kenny's adventures. "I can tell by the way you walk and your gait that something pleasant has happened. Tell me about it. Those girls at the pizza parlor?" "You're spot on! The same girls, and the gang really clicked this time; they're becoming less shy and more bold. They exchanged phone numbers and plan to keep meeting there. They know I'm unavailable, so everything's good. The gang was on cloud nine heading home. Britta asked me to send her best wishes; she's doing great too and is on good terms with everyone." "That's wonderful to hear. But don't think I've forgotten your lovely gesture with that yellow rose; it came with such a sweet kiss. I've prepared another treat for you after you show me your French perfection. But don't worry, whether you pass or fail, you won't lose your treat. You can't beat a deal like that!" Patey led Kenny to the bed, open his shirt, then crawled into bed and laid her head on a pillow. She pulled her robe over her thigh and teased Kenny, saying, "I'm naked, so beg me to open it all up, in good French." It was a major distraction, but Kenny felt confident in his French skills.

Maybe because he had to manage the robe request, he kind of fumbled it a bit. He understood that Patey desired perfection; when she shook her head, it meant back to the workbench again. However, there was still the treat to look forward to. Patey slid off the bed and beckoned him toward the bathroom. There, the instructions were laid out clearly. "Like always, Kenny, don't overthink this. Your treat is not a game or a test; it's a gift just for you. I have this old porcelain tub filled with water, infused with soap and fragrances. I'll allow you to give me a bath. The robe and towel rack are right there. You will remove my robe from my naked body; keep any arousal to yourself. I will step into the tub, and you can bathe me anywhere you want, even my hair and boobs, except for my vagina area—you can move wherever you like. When you're finished, place a towel for me to stand on, and you can dry me off almost everywhere, except for my hair, which I'll handle. Once you're done, put my robe on me, not you, silly. The rest is history for you. 'Okay, you can start.'"

All good things must come to an end, but what an ending this was! Who wouldn't be thrilled? Even fantasy couldn't compare or compete. Patey's naked body carried all the fragrances of soap and bubbles, and that scent put Kenny in a trance. He was mesmerized in a euphoric stupor, almost as if Patey had to snap her fingers to wake him up to reality. Patey wondered if she had gone too far this time, but he would live, she concluded with a laugh. The fantasy reality had ended, and the ritual kiss goodbye was fulfilled. Patey asked, "Are you walking home today?" to which Kenny jokingly replied, "I'll fly on fantasy wings!"

Beyond belief, Kenny had survived. What a day he recollected! My hands touched almost every inch of her naked body—her beautiful, voluptuous form. All that soap and fragrant lather highlighted the sight of her dripping wet curves as she stood, and as I rinsed her curved body—clean-shaven genitals, every inch of her under the control of my fingertips as I dried her off. This moment will be forever branded in my brain, seared by hot flashes, impossible to describe the images.

So how am I going to report to my keen listeners about my adventure into stupor? How do I articulate my feelings, emotions, thoughts, and desires? Will they indirectly experience what my body felt? I must admit that this has happened to others in life; this is merely one episode, not the pinnacle. Why am I so obsessed on this one? Patey will always introduce new things for me to explore. There must be other episodes canned for my life to disclose. A movie doesn't end after only one scene; my life shouldn't either. These never-ending, persistent thoughts kept flooding in like relentless locomotives, wondering if there's a caboose at the end and if there is one at all. Kenny, still contemplating.

The caboose isn't the subject to ponder; Patey's action scenes are the focus for my captive audience. My gang, Mr. Woods, where and how do I begin? That will work itself out, Kenny mused. Ben came on time after a quick breakfast; the usual pleasantries aside, the entire gang was in, spot selected, and the engine stopped. "Okay guys, listen up! Don't even blink—it was awesome! If there's a better word, I'd use it. Take my advice: a woman appreciates a man's display of affection; his pensiveness is an expression. I bought a single rose. It pleased all her senses. I kissed her and dragged her inside to our chilled ale table. While drinking and chatting, Patey always continued to share stories of her encounters in other countries. Once that was over, she put her elbows on the table and leaned forward as if to listen intently, but in doing so, she revealed her boobs, seemingly bra-less; she might as well have been completely naked. Then, slyly, she asked me about my morning. She correctly guessed we had a happenstance with the pizza girls. She is so insightful, and I recounted everything that happened.

But now it gets exciting, Kenny continued. She allowed me to give her a tub bath while being stark naked. Of course, she gave me specific instructions first. As I supposed, she was completely nude under her robe. I was told to remove her robe by the tub, which was already prepared with fragranced water and bubbles. She stood there like a naked goddess, stepped into the tub, and slowly lowered herself down, the water just covering her boobs. I could wash any part of her body except for her vagina. Her hair, her tits—every inch of her was fair game except that one area. I took my time. When I was finished, she stood up, dripping wet and naked. I used the handheld shower to rinse her body of bubbles, then placed a towel for her to step onto, wiping every inch of her body except her hair and face. Once that was done, I fetched her robe and slipped it on her, and the rest is now history in my mind. She complimented me on my good manners, and we concluded my delight with a sensuous kiss. I hope I didn't miss anything. I didn't overlook the dropped jaws of the guys. Their fantasy episode tale was tantalizing enough to ignite their greedy minds for now. They're aware that talking to girls can't compare to giving a naked woman a tub bath. I'm always grateful for providing virgins with some insight into what to expect, maybe. But it unfolds in chapters like a movie or a book, leaving us hanging in the air—with no refunds or consolation prizes.

They all went to their classes overjoyed, a good feeling overwhelming them. I wish I could feel that way, but there aren't many Patey's around to acknowledge. Kenny's French clouds came, and then it all ended on a high note. Now it's time to inform Mr. Woods. But Mr. Woods is a married man; there's nothing I can say that he hasn't seen already. How can I make it thrilling for him? It doesn't seem to be an issue; he displays a keen and excited look that makes me wonder

The French Graduate

about his sex life. Not everyone marries a sexpot or a hottie. Sex is just sex, I guess. Just maybe not as colorful or episodic. Should I give him the full scoop or scale it down, perhaps ratchet it up? I'm going to watch and monitor his reactions, not like the gang who is hungry for every detail—"don't hold back anything; it's easy to relate." Mr. Woods presents a mystery, an unknown factor. Being matured and being a stud is a mysterious subject for married men. Is intelligence a clue? Even dummies have sex. Sex can't be for the obscure only. It's a mystery where Mr. Woods fits in; it's not like he's married to a porn star, with Kenny's thoughts flooding his mind.

Well, here goes the full load. "It all started with a rose," Kenny began. "What color was it?" Mr. Woods asked. Kenny replied, "Yellow," though he wondered why it mattered. "Oh, the last time it was Lavender," Mr. Woods recalled. Kenny thought to himself, "Well, he remembered."

"I kissed her and carried her to the table where we enjoyed our chilled ale again." He anticipated Mr. Woods might comment further, but he stayed silent. "Patey rested her elbows on the table and propped forward in such a way that revealed she was braless, and perhaps nude under her robe." "You could see that she was naked?" Mr. Woods inquired. "You could see?" "With a sheer robe, it's fairly easy. She's often nude; she does wear a robe with me, though. It's obvious when someone is nude."

"Okay, go on. Then what?" Kenny sensed that Mr. Woods had a taste for salacious events. He decided to continue and describe everything in vivid detail. "Just looking at her beautiful knobs was a treat, and she knew that, of course. She asked me about my day while providing a side show distraction, a show within a show. She was testing my focus under pressure. I realized it was a maneuver, and I managed to pass it. Mr. Woods gave the impression that he would have failed. I could be wrong.

"But that was only the first act; you're going to love the finale," Kenny hinted. "Would you believe, Patey filled her old Proclaim bathtub with bubbling, scented suds, all ready and waiting. She gave me detailed instructions to follow. I was to give her a tub bath, laying a towel on the floor by the tub. I would stand there and you will take off my robe, hanging it there alongside two towels—one for my body and one for my hair and face. I would step into the tub and lower myself into the bubbles. You can remove your shirt and kneel next to the tub, using that soap to give me a bath on your knees and move anywhere you need to wash. Wash anywhere you want excepting my vagina area, understand? She's fully naked, shaved clean.

The directions felt like a totaled painting—stay within the lines, and I can do that. "Just use the soap gently, and linger if you want; there's no time clock running," Patey smiled.

"Can you picture that scene?" Kenny asked Mr. Woods.

"Yes, in slow-motion frames," he confessed.

"Good, and now for the last act, frame by frame for you." Kenny watched Mr. Woods reposition himself in his chair as if not to miss a word.

"After I washed every inch of her body, her hair, Patey would express her enjoyment by occasionally raising her boobs above the bubbles, to my delight, visually. But it became evident that she was done. She rose like a goddess, dripping wet, and told me to pull the drain plug while I used the hand shower to rinse her off. Then she stepped out for me to wipe her dry. I slowly and gently wiped her body while she did her face and hair, swishing it around her head in a tuck. Patey complimented me for doing a good job, being a good listener, and exhibiting good behavior. I covered her voluptuous body with her robe, and my treat was history. Surprisingly, the ale was still cold, and she commented that it might be needed to cool me down from my high. My eventful day ended with a kiss that gave my imprimatur to the event.

The French Graduate

The rhetorical question to ask Mr. Woods was, "Well, what do you think of my Patey?"

"It was just as high for me. What a tale! You said it without missing a beat. If you don't tell me the next installment, I'll give you an 'F.' I mean it, I'm serious," he said, and they both laughed at his pun.

"Seriously, that was interesting. You should write a book," said Mr. Woods as he departed.

What else can Patey come up with? Kenny wondered. Was that my last treat? Is sex next? Is my French acceptable? Will I fail again? Will God reward or punish me? Will I die before Saturday? Is there an ending? These are all unanswered questions from a mind overflowing with thoughts. Will my life have a sequel? This was a fresh thought in Kenny's mind, but there were no fresh answers for sure. Will Saturdays be erased from the calendar? That's not logical; Saturday has been my life, my new life. I can't picture any life without Patey—lover or friend, friend or lover. Patey will always be in my life, period.

Kenny seemed to be a lamplighter, lighting everyone's wick. Everyone seems happier because of him—his smile, his charisma, whatever it is. It's contagious. His mom and dad, the gang, Britta and friends, teachers, counselors, Mr. Woods—they all seem happier. Even Kenny feels it. In Kenny's mind, the dots all connect back to Patey. She radiates happiness, always with a good disposition, never negative. She lights me up, and I pass it on. But there is one kink in this wheel: Mom is that kink. Mom hates Patey, so I try to keep them apart. The thing is, Patey loves Mom unconditionally. My job is to find a solution. Somehow, this one is on me, not on Patey.

Classes are good; French is good, if not better. But good does not come easy. It does not come by a magical switch; it takes effort to push it forward—a power, like the wind on a sail, propelling it forward and a rudder to set its course. However, the goals in life are not on a straight course. A good navigator will tack it to his advantage to reach his destination. Kenny must try to solve his dilemma. Is he up to the task? You'll see.

How much easier a day goes on a happy note, not flat. Kenny tries to use his French more—in class and with friends—with the exception of home. He tries not to be pompous or ostentatious with his French. His gang does not mind, and they even start to use words of salutation like "hello," "good morning," and "goodbye" in French—things like that. They say it with a chuckle and are always eager to add to their repertoire. It adds a little color to their character, they think. Needless to say, it adds to the saying, "Where did the time go?" and "Time flies when you're having fun." So, there goes the day zinging by, and good Lord, it's Saturday again. The day when everything goes in slow motion for Kenny, and there are times he wishes he had a pause button to push at the right moment—the right scene at the right place on Patey's body. But wishes are for dreamers, and learning is more practical.

Morning just fell into place—no drama, no drum roll. Plain English greetings for Mom and French greetings to the gang. Surprisingly, they replied in French and felt proud doing it. This day was also the gang's day with the pizza girls. Kenny told them that if the girls were there, as they said, they were on their own, and he wasn't a babysitter. "I kept my promise; it's your game now. I'll be there as an umpire to make sure you guys behave, not as a babysitter but as a referee," Kenny said half-jokingly.

"You mean we can't play a hole-in-one or score a touchdown?" Allen quipped.

"No," Kenny replied, "girls are not a game. Treat them with respect."

This was all said moments ago, and it was speculative because the turn ahead was to the pizza parlor. The girls were only speculation, too. Ben parked and decided to go in to see if they were there or if they should sit. To their amazement and pleasure, the girls were already there. Two of the girls waved them over, and after exchanging glances with the gang, Kenny took a small chance, knowing their feelings, and joined their table. "We've got a situation we can't ignore," Kenny said, addressing the group as he brought up the idea of treating the girls instead of splitting the bill. After a quick discussion, the gang gave their approval. "I know we usually go Dutch, but this time, just this once, we're treating. Please, make our day by saying yes." The girls smiled and agreed, and with that, the game was on. They laughed, joked, teased, and interacted like longtime friends. They talked about music, movies, and games, to everyone's delight. The girls gave Ben some CDs to play in the car audio. In the end, it was a given—next week was confirmed. This was by far the best ever for Ben, Allen, and Glen. Kenny enjoyed it too, but in a different way, and left them briefly to call Patey and buy a pink rose.

The gang was in the best of moods when they dropped Kenny off. He was more than eager to meet up with Patey. As usual, Patey was there, waiting just as eagerly for Kenny. He presented her with the pink rose, and she received it with gracious beauty. Patey invited him inside, and they kissed sensually and swayed a little. They then retreated to the table for some chilled ale.

As they drank their ale, Patey gave Kenny some instructive analogies about probabilities and penetrance. When she finished, Kenny expected her to ask about his day, but he was wrong. Patey excitedly asked, "Have you ever watched a movie where two lovers meet after a long absence? The girl runs to him, hops on his hips, and they kiss, swirling around?"

"Yes, many times. Why?"

"I've always wanted to do it, just once in my life. Let's do it."

"I liked it too, but I've never had a girl, so I'm game if you are. It's a delightful display of emotions."

"Okay, you stand back there. I'll be there. Be prepared for the jump."

Patey was wearing a short robe, panties, and a bra. "Here I come!" she called out. Kenny stood firm, and Patey jumped spread-eagle onto his hips. They locked lips, and he swirled her around, still kissing, still straddling, and still hugging. Patey seemed reluctant to get off, but she eventually did. They both laughed and laughed—it worked. It was a scene from a movie, all choreographed by Patey. It made both their days; it was delightful to the max.

The movie of that scene didn't end with the credits rolling—it was only the trailer; the main feature was just starting for Kenny. "I have another surprise treat for you," Patey confessed. "You remember your treat from last time—you gave me a tub bath. This time, it's the reverse: I'll give you a tub bath. Now listen again; the same rules apply. Keep any arousal in low gear. Everything is prepared again; you take off all your clothes—every bit of it—and step in, just as I did. Sit and lounge in the bubbles. I'll take off my robe and bra and do what you did to me. I will soap you everywhere discretely, so don't flaunt anything, or you're done. Is that all understood?"

"Yes," Kenny sheepishly replied. "But I'm a little embarrassed about taking all my clothes off in front of a woman and being nude. I know it's silly, but can I face away?"

"Yes, this time I expected it. But you'll get the hang of it next time—pun intended," Patey giggled.

"Now stay still while I wash your hair, doing it topless the whole time. There's a dry towel there in case I get soap in your eyes; I'll be careful. I hope you don't mind the female fragrance. Try to hide it from Mom and sneak in."

"No, I'm loving it. Smelling good is a turn-on, especially on you. Your pores, your hair, and even your breath have a fragrance."

Naturally, Kenny wanted to stay all day, but done is done, and Patey calls the shots.

Kenny seemed reluctant to stand up naked to rinse off, and Patey understood the signals. "I'll give you some space and wait for you at the table. While you wipe and change, I'll be waiting, and so will your ale." When Kenny came to the table, he smelled like the perfumes at a sample counter. Patey purred, "Mmm, you smell sexy. Want to jump kiss again?" Patey joked.

"I'd like to throw a joke at that, but I'm gun-shy to do so," Kenny quipped.

"Your quip away. I love jokes or sly remarks; they show a sharp mind, and I can take it. What was the joke?"

"Well, when you mentioned having a jump kiss, I was going to quip, 'Only if you lose some pounds.'"

"Wow, that's a nice. But are you normally suicidal?" Patey responded.

"Damn, you're good. What a comeback," Kenny had to admit.

They both laughed and high-fived. Laughing made it hard to drink their ale. This was a fun and fulfilling day for both Kenny and Patey.

Weekends are the best for thrills, while weekdays are for the encore of the script—for the gang and Mr. Woods. There's excitement in the air, thrills, a roller coaster ride, and anticipation is the essence of living. The past weekend lived up to its billing, with Patey as the main attraction, the star. Thank God there's a Sunday to settle down from the high. On Sunday, God rested, right? Kenny surmised. Everything in due time; lives go on, and Kenny is loving every square inch of Patey, wondering how much more there is to experience with her.

For all that happened, it might take a whole week to relate it to the gang and Mr. Woods. But Kenny knew that once he started, they would never let him walk away from the action scenes. So, Kenny told the gang that the best way would be for them to come to Mr. Woods' classroom, where he could shut the door for more discrete storytelling and not have to repeat it multiple times. It was a wait, but Kenny decided it would be worth it. When they finally arrived, Kenny introduced them officially, although Mr. Woods had always seen them on campus. They all sat around Mr. Woods' table, with him in his seat.

Kenny began by telling them that they wouldn't want to miss any square inch of the story, giving them a hint about what it would involve. There was no need to embellish anything—there was enough material to fill a book. Just sticking to the script would be salacious enough. How could he forget anything? It was only this Saturday. Kenny started from the beginning: he bought her a pink rose, which she was eagerly expecting. She pulled him in, and they kissed cozily, then moved on to the chilled ale.

Patey talked about many things to enlighten him. To his surprise, Patey wanted to act out that movie scene where two lovers who have been apart for a while meet, with the girl running to him, hopping on his hips, and kissing and twirling around in delight. That's exactly what they did, and it worked. They laughed and joked about it, vowing to do it again another time. It was fun and fun. A little breathless, they sat down for more ale to recover. But that was just the entrée; the main dish was the treat.

Patey guided him to the bathroom to reveal her script. She asked if he remembered last week and how could he forget? She said it would be the reverse of him giving her a tub bath—she would give him one instead. The tub was prepared with bubbles and fragrant water up to his neck. He was to take off all his clothes in front of her and lounge in the tub. But he had to admit, he was too embarrassed and asked if he could turn away to do it. She anticipated this and agreed, and he quickly undressed and got in.

The French Graduate

Patey took off her robe and bra, leaving only her panties on. She washed almost every part of his body with a warning not to flaunt any arousal, or he'd be done. She took her time washing his hair and body, not rushing it. It was exhilarating to the max. When she was finished, he stood up, still naked, and she understood his shyness. She went outside to let him wipe off and dress. She was so insightful. They finished the ale and toasted to the treat in style.

The treat was not related to any failure in his French. Patey knew what she wanted first and wasn't too often deterred by his French flirtation. As always, Patey considered Mom in her script.

We now normally kiss with a little passion as a goodie. And that's the end, my friends. Enjoy, and stay tuned for the sequels. It seemed that everyone wanted to be the stand-in actor or stuntman for obvious reasons. It was a good screenplay session.

"Well, do I get an 'A+' for my storytelling?" Kenny asked Mr. Woods.

"I'll give you the 'A' for now and the plus when I get the next chapter," Mr. Woods replied.

The door that had kept them in suspense was opened, and they all left for home.

From now on, each coming week is a repeat of the last, except for Patey's innovative escapades with Kenny. No one doubts Patey's catalog of events and treats now, and they all think it will culminate in sex. Only Mr. Woods doubts it. Kenny has his doubts, too, for unknown reasons, but he takes it one week at a time with a "let's see" attitude.

Cutting to the chase, Kenny buys a white rose. As he approaches the door, it feels odd; Patey is usually there. He knocks, and she invites him in. He steps inside with the rose in hand and sees Patey back at the table with a big, wide smile.

He says, "Hi, babe," but as he does, he has a flash of what she intends to do—hip kiss him again. He holds his elbows high so she can straddle his hips cleanly. Knowing what to expect helps; it goes well, better than expected. Patey is pleased.

"Is this going to be the norm?" Kenny asks.

"No," Patey replies. "The last time was all choreographed; this time, it's more spontaneous and well-played out. Next time will be super perfect—you'll see."

Then, they move on to the chilled ale, this time with a lemon twist on each glass. With the white rose to the side and occasionally intertwined fingers while talking, they discuss his thoughts, subjects of interest, and his dreams.

It is Patey's turn to introduce a subject. "Kenny, males have an inherent attraction to females by nature. Arousal is necessary to facilitate intercourse. It's natural to be aroused because of attraction, but when it doesn't directly lead there, having a hard-on for other events is not required. A slight arousal is normal; full-on, no. Your mind should control the situation. As in my bath and yours, it was sensual, not sexual. You are expected to know the difference. If you are too shy, it may shrink instead, so not being super shy is better in the long run, pun intended. When that moment arrives, you will know and perform accordingly, trust me."

Kenny only wished he had known earlier, but lessons don't come easy.

So here we are, just you and me, with nothing but a good French proposition to get me to the moment of the request: sex. The last opportunity was waved off due to time and Mom. This time will be different; I will prevail, contrived in the mind of Kenny the Optimistic. Little does he know, Patey is determined to keep him a virgin for reasons of her own. Patey led Kenny to the edge of the bed, removed his shirt, took her robe off, and, as she turned around, told

The French Graduate

Kenny to remove her bra; she crawled onto the bed wearing only panty to a pink pillow, lavender sheets, and in a seductive pose, begged for a proposal. Kenny was enthralled by Patey's bare knockers and found it hard to focus. He tried to propose with all the determination he could muster, but it was for nothing. Patey always found some small mistake, like forgetting to cross a "T" or something getting lost in translation—maybe this time because Kenny was too busy staring to get his words right. Patey got off the bed and put on her robe, but not tieing it, went to Kenny, turned him to face her and sat him down on the bed, his face level with her breast. She leads him forward into her boobs on both sides of his face and snuggles him, her hands around his head. He kissed her belly and hugged her body as she pressed and wiggled it in his face. The pleasure was indescribable. Almost nothing could compare to Kenny, with nothing to compare it with.

As Patey pulled her boobs away from his face, Kenny was reluctant to let go, but just moving back to view her breast was a treat in itself. Shirtless, Kenny was led to the bathroom. The room of return. Patey again dictated instructions and the program. For your failure treat, we are going to shower together. Remember the code of conduct, the protocols, the caveats, the arousal lecture, and the respect. I will take my panty off and my robe, and start the shower. You will undress and step in with me. We soap each other discreetly and enjoy the moment and exuberance together. We rinse off with water, dry with the towel, and off you go to Mom. Any complaints will be non-existent and non-refundable, Patey laughed. The kiss goodbye topped it off.

Not that Patey was running out of treats, but the days were running short until school ended with graduation, and Kenny was chosen to be the valedictorian speaker. It was easy for Kenny; he had straight A's and an A+ in French. He was well-liked by everyone—girls gave him catcalls in admiration, Britta drooled over him, and his gang respected him. Everything was good. His mom and dad were so proud, and the best was saved for last: Patey would be ecstatic.

But there is still a conundrum to solve: the kink in the wheel—Mom. Will it work for her as well? This is something I must solve by all means. Another kink is Mr. Woods. He knows that after graduation, I'll be gone, out into the world, out of his class, and no more salacious stories to enjoy. He confides in me his suspicion that my relationship with Patey is unique and special. According to him, from the way I've described it, Patey does not intend to give me sex but is seducing me to learn French. She is mentoring me to master French by asking me to beg for it in French to get sex. No matter how well I use French, she will and did refuse me. She seduced me with the expectation of getting sex and gave me treats to urge me on in a grand learning experience. But Mr. Woods didn't believe that I was totally oblivious.

Yes, it did dawn on me eventually. But when I consider what I was to what I am, I'm in. Patey mentored me to be a better person, to be a man, to have emotional feelings, to respond to lovemaking, to kiss, to remove a bra or panty, to understand how it feels to hold and touch a woman, and to be gentle and thoughtful. The list is endless. It was fate that I met Patey; our DNA met each other in a time capsule. She is my friend for life. I could never say goodbye to her—I would cry an ocean and be a total mess. I will always be connected to her like an unsevered umbilical cord. Even if and when I get married, she comes with me as a total package, not as a sexual lover but as a sensuous friend, a mutual soul. Life does not have an autocorrect button.

Okay, this is it—graduation is now front and center. There's so much activity, like a beehive, with bustling excitement in the air and even an aroma to it. Everyone is energized and fully charged. The gang is graduating, too, each heading toward their own future destinies. Moms and dads, friends and neighbors, flowers, cards, gifts, outfits (and even "ensembles" if there is such a thing), curlers and lipstick working their magic. This day of transformation will live forever in their souls. Such was the case for Kenny.

The French Graduate

Kenny's mom and dad, dressed up as any proud parents would, arrived early to get front-row seats, program in hand. The seats filled up quickly, with much chatter and nursing. The usual decorum and ambiance of any graduation prevailed. Then, the hum of a microphone came on, a speaker gave the welcome speech, and there was a secular thanks to God. Several speakers delivered their pieces, and the last song was sung. The anticipated announcement came: the valedictorian speaker was Kenny Cannon. Mom and Dad led the chorus of applause; then silence fell as everyone listened to Kenny's speech. Standing at the podium in cap and gown, Kenny used the time to adjust the mic to take a quick look for Patey. He already knew where his mom and dad were seated, so he looked elsewhere. Though he didn't see her, he knew she was there; she would never miss his graduation for anything.

Kenny looked directly at the crowd, knowing he could never spot her out there. He had to deliver his speech directly. He didn't need notes, as he had composed and rehearsed it thoroughly. He expressed gratitude to all who had dedicated themselves to his education and to everyone else, year after year. When he was done, he didn't wait for applause to interrupt his ending. In very fluent French, Kenny gave praise and heartfelt thanks to his beloved Patey by name and for her role as his mentor up to this point. He acknowledged that he would not be here without her and ended with a simple, "Thank you, Patey." Only a few understood what Kenny said in French, but he concluded with a heartfelt "Thank you all for this wonderful day." Mom and Dad, elated, applauded with the crowd.

Each graduate was assigned a spot in the arena for parents, family, and friends, as posted in the program. Kenny wanted to get there as quickly as possible to see Patey, knowing she would be there. As he approached, he saw Patey in a pantsuit, waving at him. He sensed what she was going to do, smiled in approval, and waited for her joyful sprint toward him, gown be damned. They kissed like lovers, and he whirled her around with joy. He let her down, but she continued bouncing, hugging, and giggling with excitement, congratulating and thanking him for the acknowledgments.

Lost in the excitement, Mom arrived ahead of the rest. Upon seeing Patey hugging and kissing Kenny, she erupted in a frenzy. In front of everyone, she screamed, "You fucking whore, how dare you even come here! I warned you to keep away from my son, you bitch. Get the 'F' out of here, you bitch! I don't want to see you again, ever!"

Patey placed her hand on Kenny's shoulder, smiled, and whispered, "It's okay, don't worry about it. I understand." Then, she quietly left the arena. Kenny carried on as if nothing had happened, and the congratulations continued until the end.

The next morning began with a celebratory breakfast, almost like a buffet—take as much as you want. Mom had gotten up extra early to prepare it. Happy as can be, with only three people there, the breakfast was more symbolic, with the possibility that someone might pop in. It didn't matter; they feasted and chatted, mainly about graduating and the future. Mom expressed how proud she was of her brilliant son and his magnificent speech, which had received a good round of applause.

"But you also spoke in French. You know I don't understand French, so what were you saying?" Mom asked.

Kenny lowered his fork to his plate, leaned back in his chair, and began to think. Is this the time, the moment of truth? Can I fix this issue now? You've thought about this countless times—speak up or forever regret it. He pondered whether she would understand, whether she would forgive him. This is my moment, he thought. "Mom... there is something we need to settle. Just sit and listen with an open mind. Don't interrupt, please. My speech in French was to thank Patey, the girl you hate—the girl in the red convertible and at my graduation. Her name, if you've forgotten, is Patey."

"You mean that whore? How could you? She's no good; she's just a sex worker. I told you and her to stay away from you. Have you been seeing her? Tell me the truth."

The French Graduate

Kenny leaned back and quietly listened, almost looking away, but made a glance at Dad, who remained silent, not wanting to take sides. "Yes, Mom. I have never stopped seeing and meeting Patey. I've been with her for months and will never, ever stop, even if my life depended on it. I love her in a special way. She's the best thing that's come into my life. Yes, you might call her a prostitute, but she is the most wonderful person I've ever known. She is brilliant—born in France to a wealthy family, went to university there, studied philosophy and psychology, traveled to many countries, and speaks perfect, fluent French. I hate to tell you this, but I was failing grades and had an 'F' in French. I didn't care; I was in a rut and most likely not going to get a diploma. I was consumed with sex; I was a virgin. I wanted to break my virginity, the root of my apathy and ambivalence. So, the gang and I went to a brothel here in town."

At this revelation, both Mom and Dad leaned forward to listen more intently.

The brothel was discrete and tucked away, secluded from the rest of the world. We had no clue about anything else—we went there for one reason: sex, to get laid. But when we realized we didn't have enough money, they threw us out—everyone except me. One prostitute, Patey, took an interest in me. She had a monitor and liked what she saw about me. She took no money, only took an interest in me, she said that I was different in some strange way, maybe my DNA. a sense about me, she did not seduce me with sex, instead, she asked me about myself and my perspectives, my DNA beliefs of intelligence, family, gang, my preset ambivalence, my low grades, an "F" in French, and my virginity holding me back. Patey listened very intently, and she seemed to notice something in about me that caught her mind that I did not know at that time. By listening to the things I said, she concluded that I had potential that I wasn't stupid like I thought. What she decided was to mentor me—not just through conversations but through the promise of sex. She had her own apartment, and we would meet there. I had her address and number. She told me if I ever wanted sex, I'd have to come back and ask for it—in perfect French. She dangled the idea of sex, using it as motivation. But each time, after all my studying, she told me my French still wasn't good enough. I studied and studied, trying to reach proficiency, but it was never enough. I'm still a virgin. Month after month, she would refuse, but instead of leaving me frustrated, she taught me lessons about how to act, how to respect women, how to treat women and many things sensual, not sexual. She loves you and understands where you're coming from, you are just like her mom. That is why she only smiles at what you do because any mother would do it too. She sends me home on time out of respect for my mom, not just for me. Patey honestly loves and cares about you, my mother. No matter what you've said or done, she understands. To love me is, in a way, to love her too.

By the time Kenny finished speaking, Mom was in tears, sobbing almost uncontrollably. She was overwhelmed, flashing back to everything she'd said and done. "Ugh," she cried out, "I'm so sorry, so ashamed of how I acted, especially in public." She wiped her face, trying to regain composure. "From everything you've said, we owe her too. I have to apologize and make amends," she said to Kenny. "Where can I meet her?" Kenny sighed. "I can arrange a meeting, but don't expect to apologize—she won't let you. I know her too well. You can try, but it won't change anything. In fact, you'll probably end up falling in love with her when you meet her. Here's her address and number. I'll give her a heads-up that you're coming. Is 10 a.m. on Monday good for you?"

Kenny's mom put on a nice dress, fluffed her hair a bit, and set off to meet Patey. Kenny had given her the time. Patey figured that Mom might feel a bit uncomfortable inside her apartment, so she suggested meeting outside instead. There was a small lawn with a bench where they could sit. Patey recognized the car and waved as Mom approached. As they met, Patey extended her hand warmly. "Hi, Mrs. Cannon, or can I call you Sylvia? I'm Patey, as you probably already know." "Yes, I do, and yes, Sylvia is fine. I came to..." "Sylvia, if you try to apologize, I'm going to break down and cry, so please don't. Don't feel bad about what happened—any mother would have

The French Graduate

done the same. Kenny is the most wonderful, talented, intelligent, sensitive, and well-mannered person I know, and I credit you for that. I miss my mom so much, and I was hoping you might let me be your friend, maybe even like a daughter?" "You're so sweet for saying that," Sylvia replied, her voice softening. "Kenny warned me you'd be disarming and lovable, and he was right. I can see why he loves you, and I think I will, too. Welcome to the family, Patey." "Can we hug, Mom?" Patey asked, her voice almost shy. Kenny's mom felt her heart melt. "I never had a daughter," she mused as they embraced tightly, feeling the warmth of connection. When they finally parted, both women promised to keep in close touch. Kenny would make sure of that.

So, how does this saga end? Kenny has secured a scholarship to a prestigious university, while Patey is heading toward a teaching role at a university herself. Mom and Dad, now empty nesters, remain in touch with Kenny and Patey. As for Kenny and Patey, when they had to shift the way they were together, it was tough, like letting go of something precious. But it wasn't a goodbye or a real parting. They simply needed to change the romantic part of their relationship, something they both knew would happen, though it was hard to face.

Even though it hurt, they understood their bond went beyond romance. They promised to stay close as friends—friends who still cared deeply for each other, just in a different way. Their love was built on trust and respect, and neither of them was leaving the other behind. Patey never doubted Kenny's care for her, and Britta, who knew about their history, never felt like Patey was a threat.

Some of you might wonder what happened with Kenny and Britta. Though their first spark didn't lead anywhere, sometimes love works out later. After Kenny and Patey shifted to being close friends, he and Britta reconnected. This time, things worked out, and now they're happily married, showing that love can bloom when the time is right.

As for Kenny and Patey, they still remain loving friends—connected in a way that no distance or life change could break.

About the Author

I am who I am—no more, no less. My life is made up of many different experiences. I spent 30 years as a General Contractor, building homes and working on various projects. I also served for 13 years in the National Guard, where I reached the rank of Sergeant First Class.

For two years, I worked in Real Estate, learning about buying and selling homes. I have two U.S. Patents that show my interest in creating new things. I wrote and copyrighted a song and enjoy singing Country and Western music, winning many amateur contests and even appearing on TV.

In addition to my construction work, I have built boats and created a treehouse and deck. I love the outdoors and enjoy hunting, fishing, hiking, and sailing. Each of these activities has shaped who I am today.

Kenneth Chang

The End

www.ingramcontent.com/pod-product-compliance
Ingram Content Group UK Ltd.
Pitfield, Milton Keynes, MK11 3LW, UK
UKHW041854250225
455528UK00005B/21